WINTER'S WARRIOR

THE WICKED WINTERS BOOK 13

SCARLETT SCOTT

Winter's Warrior

The Wicked Winters Book 13

All rights reserved.

Copyright © 2021 by Scarlett Scott

Published by Happily Ever After Books, LLC

Edited by Grace Bradley

Cover Design by Wicked Smart Designs

This book or any portion thereof may not be reproduced or used in any manner whatsoever without the express written permission of the publisher except for the use of brief quotations in a book review.

The unauthorized reproduction or distribution of this copyrighted work is illegal. No part of this book may be scanned, uploaded, or distributed via the Internet or any other means, electronic or print, without the publisher's permission. Criminal copyright infringement, including infringement without monetary gain, is punishable by law.

This book is a work of fiction and any resemblance to persons, living or dead, or places, events, or locales, is purely coincidental. The characters are productions of the author's imagination and used fictitiously.

For more information, contact author Scarlett Scott.

www.scarlettscottauthor.com

For all the readers who have found comfort in my happily ever afters in uncertain times.

PROLOGUE

EAST LONDON, 1815

It had taken three of her brother's guards to carry the felled giant from the streets and settle him in Caro's bed. But after he regained consciousness and began to fight, it had required five of them to help her tie the thrashing monster to the posts so she could tend him.

"Bloody madman," cautioned Randall as Caro secured the man's left wrist.

"Touched in the 'ead," counseled Hugh with a grunt as he narrowly escaped a swinging right fist before catching the man's arm and holding it to the post.

Good thing she was a bloody expert at securing prisoners. That was what spending her entire life in a gaming hell did to a girl. The beast would not escape a Caro Sutton knot.

"If he is mad, we will send him on his way," she promised, slipping around the bed to tie his other wrist as Bennet, Timothy, and Anthony held the man's legs.

"Sutton is going to rip out our guts and feed them to 'is dogs when 'e gets a sniff of this, miss." The warning, issued by Bennet, was an exaggeration.

Likely.

"I have never seen Jasper feeding entrails to his dogs yet," she said calmly, finishing the knot.

The man suddenly roared, half-insensate yet still struggling for his life.

She laid a gentle hand on his brow, which was matted with blood. "Calm yourself, sir. I only aim to help."

"I'll kill you," the man growled, thrashing some more.

It was impossible to tell if he was awake or in the grips of violent delirium. His eyes had swelled closed. The beating he had received had been merciless. There was the distinct possibility that he was also drunk, though she did not smell spirits on him. She had seen more than her share of sotted fools getting beaten and robbed in the alleys around The Sinner's Palace over the years. 'Twould be nothing new.

When she had first come across him in the alley behind her family's gaming hell, she had believed he was dead. A closer examination had proven otherwise; his chest had been rising and falling. That had been when she'd fetched Randall, Hugh, and Bennet. But from the moment she had first touched him, she had known instinctively there was something different about this man.

Her reluctant patient aimed another kick at Bennet and Timothy, landing a boot in the latter's abdomen. Timothy fell on his arse, clutching his belly and gasping for breath.

"Damn it," she grumbled.

Fortunately, she was accustomed to unruly men in need of healing. She tended to her brothers whenever there was a fight involving knives, fists, pistols, or sometimes all three at once—the Suttons were a bloodthirsty lot. There was no other solution when a man was out of his head as this one was. She was going to have to pour some laudanum down the poor cove's throat.

"Hold his head still for me, Randall," she ordered, fetching the bag she always kept at the ready and plucking the vial she required from it. "But take care where you touch him. We don't want to give him further injuries."

"If 'e bites me, I ain't going to be 'appy," the guard said.

A few months ago, her brother Rafe had accidentally bitten Randall's finger instead of the leather strap he'd been meant to gnaw on whilst she had stitched up a particularly vicious knife wound. Randall had not forgotten. Nor had he entirely forgiven Caro, even if he did favor her over all her siblings.

Caro did not fool herself for the reason. If the men were on the wrong end of a knife stick, they wanted to be certain she would be at their sides. The whispers circulating about her in the hell—that she could heal anyone—had not been aided by her natural inclination toward the medicinal. Nor all the treatises she spent each night reading until the stub of her candle flickered out.

"He shan't bite you," she told Randall, drawing nearer as the man continued to thrash and shout curses. "As long as your hold remains firm, that is."

Randall glared at her, but he did as she asked, dutifully holding her patient still as she held the vial to his lips and forced the laudanum into his mouth. Just to be certain he would swallow—for there was no telling with a man in his condition—she pinched his nostrils together. He made a choking sound but complied.

When she was satisfied he had swallowed enough of the liquid to calm him, she turned to the three men at his feet. "Hold him still for me, lads."

CHAPTER 1

His only memories were of a witch trying to kill him.

She had cast a spell over him, until he felt as if he were weighed down by boulders and had been unable to move. Then, she had forced a bittersweet potion down his throat until the darkness claimed him.

As he pondered it now, he was sure it had been the delirium of the fever Caro said had raged through him after she had found him, beaten nearly to death, with a pistol wound in his upper arm. Fortunately, the ball had passed cleanly through, but the infection that had set in after she'd stitched him up had almost been the end of him.

And the source of those terrible nightmares, which still clawed at him every night when he fell asleep.

But it was morning, light shining through the edges of the window dressings, and the bustle of the street below telling him it was past time to rise. His stomach growled, as if in competition with the din of the voices of the men and women and the clattering of drays passing in the street.

Hunger was a good sign. It meant his broken body was healing.

Too bad his mind continued to be utter rot.

He threw back the bedclothes and rose, shucking the nightshirt the glowering fellow named Randall had helped him to don the evening before. Removing the shirt required great care and patience, for his injured arm remained difficult to move. Now that he was at last feeling like a man instead of an invalid, however, it was worth the risk. He had been longing to wear the shirt and trousers which were neatly folded and awaiting him across the room.

When Caro had brought him the clothing a few days ago, he had not yet been strong enough to don them. But each day, he regained more of his ability. And when he had risen this morning, he had decided it was at last time to make an effort.

He may not recall a single, damned detail about who he was or why he had found himself nearly dead behind a gaming hell called The Sinner's Palace, but today, he was going to wear some cursed rigging as if he were an ordinary chap.

He winced as he struggled to remove his wounded arm from the sleeve of the nightshirt, then cried out as the stitches pulled. But he was determined. Biting his lip hard, he pulled his arm free, then slid the entire garment over his head.

The door to the chamber flew open and Caro stepped over the threshold, bearing a tray.

He froze, and the one portion of his anatomy which seemed to have remained unaffected by the injuries he had endured went rigid. Forgetting himself, he attempted to clamp his hands over his cockstand, and howled in pain as the stitches in his arm pulled once more.

Wide, hazel eyes were upon him. Upon *that* particular part of him.

"Oh bloody hell," she said, nearly sending the tray's contents to the floor. "Forgive me. I had no notion you were bare-arsed."

The heavy door had already closed on its own momentum at her back.

They were alone.

Damnation, she was beautiful. Through the haze of pain, through the agony of fire burning in his arm, he recognized it. The shock of his hasty movement had made his cock soften, but it did not remain so for long.

It never did in this woman's presence. Miss Caro Sutton was an angel. He was convinced of it.

"Apologies, Caro," he managed, standing there awkwardly, trying not to admire the flush creeping over her or the glistening strands of auburn in her chestnut hair.

"It is I who should be sorry," she said, her husky voice falling around him like a warm caress. "I ought to have knocked. In my haste to bring you some sustenance, I assumed you would be abed and…dressed."

"I was about to be," he said wryly, nodding toward the stack of clothing.

The place where the bullet had passed through his flesh still throbbed, but the woman before him had a way of soothing even the greatest of pains. Ever since he had arisen to her lovely, concerned face hovering over him, he had found himself strangely comforted by her presence.

Indeed, over the course of the time she had spent nursing him back to health, he had become hopelessly taken with her. At least, he thought that was what this strange warmth was in his chest, this need he had for her, which burst forth, uncontrollable and overwhelming.

The devil of it was, without his memory, there was

nothing he could do with the feelings churning inside him. He could already be wed to another. He could be anyone. *Hell*, he still did not know what he looked like. For all he knew, he was bracket-faced, and a goddess like Caro would never look twice at him were she not nursing him back to health.

"I am not accustomed to you being able to move about with such freedom," she said, averting her gaze as she placed the tray upon a table. "I am well pleased to see you out of bed."

Greedily, he watched her every movement, admiring the way her gown clung to her bosom, the swell of her hips, the creaminess of her skin. He should probably return to the bed and cover himself, but he did not want to move, lest she flee.

Over the last few days, as he had become increasingly coherent, his mind clearing and his body regaining strength, she had been more skittish than usual. On edge, it seemed to him, as if there were some burden weighing upon her.

"Have you told your siblings I am here?" he asked her, wondering if the secrecy surrounding his presence was what had her so prickly or if it was merely him.

Over the course of the time she had spent tending to him, she had revealed they were staying in her family's gaming hell, The Sinner's Palace. Although her family's guards had helped her to bring him here to her rooms, they were loyal to her and had kept her secret. Her very protective siblings would not have been pleased to know their sister had brought a stranger into their midst. One she was hiding in her private room, in her *bed*. He still had not discovered where she was sleeping.

Now that he was well enough to hoist himself out of bed, he had to address the question. It was deuced unfair for Caro to be deprived of her own chamber because of him, a stranger she had rescued from death. He owed her a debt of tremendous magnitude.

"I will tell them soon," she said, moving so that her back was to him as she fussed with the items on the tray. "I was waiting until you were well enough. I'll not have an injured man forced to endure an inquisition."

She spoke well for a woman who lived in a gaming hell.

Or at least, he thought she did. There were some things which seemed to make sense in his foggy mind. The notion of this soft-spoken, gentle, intelligent woman in the East End was not one of them.

"You will tell them today," he said. "I'll not keep you from your rooms any longer. I am well enough to go."

But as he said the words, a wave of dizziness hit. He stumbled to the side. *Christ*, mayhap he had done too much, too soon. Or perhaps it was the question of where he would go when he left his temporary lodgings here. He was no one, with no money, no memories, no name.

Caro was at his side in an instant, her arms around his waist, guiding him back to the bed. "You still need time to heal."

Her sweet scent teased his senses. Floral, he thought. Lavender? Rose? He had not asked, and his muddled mind could not be sure he even knew the distinction between the two, though the words appeared readily enough.

He forgot he was naked as a babe as she helped him to settle on the mattress.

Until he glanced down at her and realized she was carefully looking in the other direction, the flush still kissing her cheeks. "Thank you," he said, aware of the manner in which his large form must tax her smaller frame.

But she was resilient, Caro, and capable, too.

With a stern air, she flipped the bedclothes over his lap. "You are not strong enough to be wandering, but next time I will be certain to announce myself before entering, and you, sir, will be certain to be clothed."

It was a reprimand, he knew, but coming from Caro, it possessed little bite. He wondered what sort of man he was. Honorable or a rogue? A gentleman or a scoundrel? Was he kind and considerate? What if he had a woman at home? He had never considered that possibility before.

His body certainly had a mind of its own, and it wanted the woman before him.

"Aye, Caro," he said, attempting a gentle nod. Moving too strenuously still produced the devil of a headache thanks to the beating his old knowledge box had taken.

He wished he knew who had attacked him and why. Caro had told him it was a miracle he was not dead, and he believed her. He must have been in a bad way. About to croak.

But it was difficult indeed to comprehend himself in danger, when now he was ensconced in the softness of her bed, the seductive floral notes of her scent, those hazel eyes pinned on him, her hands fussing with his hair. Sweeping a lock gently from his forehead.

Christ, had anyone shown him such care?

He could not remember, but he thought not.

"How are you feeling today?" she asked him, frowning.

He did not like when she stopped smiling, for he knew from experience that her expression meant she was concerned. Worrying. Usually, over him. He did not know why, or what he had done to produce such fretting.

"I feel like I want your smile," he blurted, and then regretted his tongue's haste.

He was strangely adrift, uncertain of who he was, what he would ordinarily say. There remained the questions, as ever, gnawing away at him, filling him with guilt.

"My smile?" She obliged him by giving him a bright,

teasing grin. "And here I thought you would be wanting to break your fast."

The scents on the tray she had brought with her reached him. His stomach growled. "I cannot tell you how pleased I am to be beyond broth and gruel."

"I can well imagine." She flitted away from his bedside to fetch it before returning and placing it carefully upon his lap. "Broth and gruel are detestable. I was sick once, and my sister spooned bone broth down my throat until I nearly choked for fear of what would become of me. To this day, I cannot stomach broth."

If she had taken note of his incessant cockstand, straining against the bedclothes, she said nothing. He was partially ashamed for the rampant display, but also partially concerned with the need to keep her here, at his side. To ignore his body's reaction, over which he freely acknowledged he had no control. Being ill required a man to give up all hope of reining in his own anatomy. Ever since he had awoken, he'd been a prisoner of his inabilities: to remember, to move...*hell*, even to complete the simplest of tasks.

He turned his attention to the sustenance she had brought him. Coffee, eggs, a rasher of bacon, honey cakes. His stomach growled once more, but she was watching him, hovering near, her delicious scent like a continued benediction. He shifted on the bed, trying to find a more comfortable position, to seek some relief.

Finding none.

As long as she was here, within reach, casting her spell upon him, he was stripped of any chance at producing the necessary defenses. "I meant what I said, Caro. I'll not be taking your bed from you any longer."

Pink lingered in her countenance, but she busied herself with motion, as always. Caro was often a blur as she flitted from one task to the next. She never sat. Nor was she still.

She was always, forever, moving. And as someone who had been stricken with great difficulty when it came to his own movement, he appreciated it all the more. She was something akin to a butterfly, beautiful and bold, flying about him.

He would never catch her.

"You will remain here until you are well enough to go," she told him curtly as she tidied the assortment of tinctures and vials on the table at his side. "I have another place to sleep which suits me fine."

"I do not like your keeping me a secret from your family," he groused. "You must stop doing so."

Her smile was small, almost wistful. "You do not know my brothers. If you did, you would be thankful for this respite. Eat now, lest your food grow cold."

What choice had he? He lifted his fork and began to devour the plate she had brought him, trying his utmost to distract himself from unworthy thoughts. Thoughts that involved hauling her across his lap, sending the tray to the floor, and kissing her breathless.

* * *

"You must tell your brothers soon, Caro."

The firm, low edict of her patient hit her.

She stiffened, turning back to him, distracted from her task of tidying the bedside table with its assorted tinctures and vials. The wickedly handsome, green-eyed stranger Caro had saved from the alley behind The Sinner's Palace was a man she had not previously met. But he was one she had heard of on many occasions.

Living in the East End, a Sutton, ever aware of her family's greatest foes—the wicked Winters—how could she not? Oh, it had taken some days for his bruises to abate. For the swelling and the discoloration—blue to purple to green—to subside. But once it had, the truth had been impossible to ignore, just as his identity was.

"I will tell them when the time is right and you are well enough to face them," she assured him gently, hating herself for perpetuating the lie, although she knew she must.

In truth, her eldest brother, Jasper, had discovered her secret within hours of the man's arrival at The Sinner's Palace. As her brother Rafe was fond of saying, not even a mouse could fart in their gaming hell without Jasper being aware of it.

Jasper had taken one look at her mysterious stranger after he had discovered her secret and had recognized him.

"Gavin Winter, as I live and breathe," Jasper had muttered upon viewing her sleeping patient. "Of all the fucking luck."

Her heart had sunk, for she had already developed a bond with the man she had found bruised, bloodied, shot, and beaten nearly to death that day.

"We must tell the Winters then," she had reluctantly acknowledged. "They will be wondering where he is, worrying over him."

"Not yet," Jasper had countered with the devil's own grin. "Give me some time, Caro, whilst I decide what's best."

Caro shook herself from the memory and surveyed Gavin now. He was diabolically handsome, even bruised and battered. It was said he was stronger than a giant, and he certainly possessed the height and size to convince her of the veracity of the words. Though it was difficult to think her gentle patient capable of such feats now, he was London's greatest prizefighter, a man who had defeated all the opponents he had faced with his fists.

A man she was deceiving. Their every interaction was a betrayal, each day cutting deeper than the last. She shuddered to think of what would happen if he ever discovered the truth.

"I am not afraid to face your brothers now, if you will allow it," Gavin told her, before forking some eggs into his mouth.

His appetite had returned, which was an excellent sign. He had nearly consumed the entire plate she had brought for him. The sight of him, color in his cheeks, his body on the mend, heartened her.

Unbidden, the sight which had greeted her upon her entrance to the chamber rose in her mind. His chest was broad and lightly covered in whorls of dark hair, so much more beautiful now that he was moving and filled with life than when he had been bedridden and still. His abdomen was flat and well-defined with cords of muscle. His legs were long. But it had been another portion of his anatomy which had stolen her gaze and forced the heat into her face and the tingling low in her belly.

If Jasper or the rest of her brothers found out she had seen Gavin Winter naked as the day he was born, and that she had seen his cock, they would be furious. And furious Suttons… Well, they were decidedly dangerous. She would not wish her irate brothers upon her worst enemy, let alone Gavin.

Heavens, her ears were going hot, and so was the rest of her, just from recalling how splendidly formed the man was.

"You cannot face them just now," she forced herself to say, before turning back to the bedside table and pretending to tidy once more.

It was easier to look at bottles and ointments than it was to watch Gavin Winter eat his breakfast. Partially because the bedclothes had slipped low on his waist once more. Partially because she did not want him to see her discomfiture, which was caused by a combination of the effect he had upon her and the lies she was telling him.

"Then have a seat, at the very least, if you'll not allow me to speak to them. I'll not have you going about the room, righting the mess I have made, when it is your own. To say nothing of the manner in which I have overtaken your rooms. There is a word for this, I believe. A right fancy one. Begins with a u…"

"Usurping," she finished for him, and quite easily, too.

Jasper, as the eldest, had seen all their siblings educated when their finances had finally allowed for the expense. Caro had an affinity for the medicinal and for words both.

"Yes," he agreed. "That is the bloody one. I'll not keep you from your bed any longer."

Reluctantly, she turned back to face him, trying her utmost to keep her gaze upon his face instead of all the masculine skin revealed to her.

"But have you anywhere else to go?" she pressed, hating herself as she asked the question.

She offered it for the sake of her conscience. If Gavin Winter recalled who he was, then she could happily return him to where he belonged. She would have no other choice, and her brother Jasper would have to accept it, regardless of what it cost him.

However, if Gavin's brain remained muddled …if his memory continued to elude him, then there was no recourse save one. The one in which she already found herself hopelessly embroiled, torn between loyalty to her family and her growing feelings for Gavin. Despite the shame threatening to eat her alive, she could not deny she enjoyed having Gavin here. That she enjoyed tending to him, becoming acquainted with him.

And worse, that she was attracted to him.

His blank countenance at her query had her guilt rising once more.

"If I do have anywhere else to go, I cannot recall it," he told her around a mouthful of bacon. "But that is neither here nor there. I'll go wherever and whenever you wish. I owe you so much. More than I will ever be able to repay you, Caro."

His words were akin to the prick of a knife, scoring her skin, digging into her heart.

She had found him, it was true. And she had brought him into The Sinner's Palace and seen him tended to, his wounds cleaned and sewn shut and bandaged. However, nothing that had happened after her innocent rescue of him was worthy of Gavin Winter's gratitude.

"You needn't repay me," she denied, fidgeting with the skirt of her gown.

When her fingers could not be busy, they did not know what to do with themselves.

"But I must, Caro."

His emerald gaze called to hers, and she met it, hating the earnest tone in his voice, the absolute lack of deception.

"If you truly wish to repay me, then you will cease arguing," she said. "I insist you need some additional time to rest and regain your strength. I am staying in another chamber, one which has not been in use in some time. You needn't worry you keep me from my bed."

The memory of the brother who had occupied the chamber she was currently inhabiting made her heart give a pang. Logan's disappearance had left a great deal of pain behind. Many nights spent wondering where he had gone and what had befallen him. After a year had passed, she and her siblings had been forced to accept their brother would not be returning.

Logan's chamber had been closed ever since he had vanished, but thanks to the size of their family, it was the only spare room in the private apartments over The Sinner's Palace. It was also on the highest floor, which was why Caro had chosen to take over the room herself.

Carrying Gavin to her chamber had required far fewer steps for the guards who had hauled him from the alley on her behalf. Given the closeness of their family, it was nothing short of a small miracle that she and Jasper had managed to keep Gavin's presence a secret for as long as they had.

Gavin finished his breakfast and used a napkin on his mouth.

To Caro's shame, her gaze was drawn there, to his lips. She found herself wondering what they would feel like moving over hers. And then she reminded herself why she should never allow such a longing to take hold.

The reasons were many.

"I cannot deny I enjoy being in your bed," that wicked mouth of his said.

Bloody blue blazes.

She was hot once more, and she could not deny the answering ache between her thighs.

"Mr.—" She cut herself off abruptly, realizing that in her dudgeon, she had been about to call him *Mr. Winter* when she was not supposed to know his name. "*Sir.*"

"Begging your pardon, Caro." Gavin flushed—his neck going red along with the tips of his ears. "I… *Hell.* A man wakes up with no memory and no manners, it would seem. I hope I ain't a scoundrel. I didn't mean to blurt that as I did, although it's true."

Oh, how it pained her to keep his identity from him. She was going to have to speak with Jasper, and soon.

"You needn't fret over it," she hastened to assure him. "After the blows you took to the head, it is a miracle you are alive."

"You didn't like when I said what I did," he observed.

How wrong he was. She had liked it far too much, and that was the problem.

Her fingers, still bereft of an occupation, clenched on the light muslin of her gown. "You surprised me."

"Shocked you."

Pleased me.

She cleared her throat. "Regardless of the sentiment, you needn't worry yourself on my account. Have you finished eating?"

The longer she lingered here with Gavin, that powerful chest of his on display, those emerald eyes glinting into hers, his low voice teasing and flirtatious and like a balm upon her tattered heart, the more dangerous it was for the both of them. She was deceiving this man, and Winters were the enemy, despite the fragile truce which had been recently struck between their families. Moreover, her brothers were incredibly protective of her after what had happened with Philip.

You've landed yourself in enough trouble because of one man, Caro Sutton, she told herself sternly. *No need to make it two.*

"I have finished," he said, shaking her from her tumultuous thoughts. "Breakfast was delicious, thank you."

How polite he was, aside from his flirtatious ways. She wondered if he was always thus. From her reading, she understood that blows to the head could cause all manner of reactions. Mayhap she would need to make some discreet inquiries and discover whether or not Gavin Winter was a rake and a scoundrel. If he was, avoiding him would be so much easier. And the defenses she was struggling to keep around herself would be far stronger. Taller. *Hell*, after Philip, they would be insurmountable.

She moved nearer to him, taking the tray, trying not to stare at his chest but to focus instead upon his wound. "It is healing nicely. Have you soreness?"

He tentatively moved his arm. She would need to snip the

stitches soon. A day or two, no more, from her assessment of the time that had passed.

"I feel as if I have known worse pain," he said. "I shall live."

She suspected he had, after the fights he had fought and won. "I am glad of it. That you shall live, of course. Not that you may have suffered worse in the past."

"You have a good heart, Caro." His gaze was earnest upon hers.

She had to look away, to break the connection. "Is there anything else you will be needing?"

"Some fresh water in the pitcher when it can be had would be lovely," he said.

And then a strange expression overtook his handsome face.

"What is the matter?" she asked, thinking he was experiencing some sudden pain to which she must tend.

"I don't think I would say lovely. Feels odd." He frowned.

Oh, how she hated herself. She did not know what manner of phrasing he would have chosen, but she did know who he was.

"I will see that Randall brings you some fresh water," she said instead of giving voice to any of the emotions truly plaguing her. "I shall check on you later, sir."

With that, she hurried from the chamber.

CHAPTER 2

*C*aro went to the kitchens first, returning the empty tray she had taken to Gavin. But she did not linger, as she ordinarily was wont to do, chatting with the cantankerous chef, who always beamed when he saw her. Instead, she left, on a mission, not stopping until she burst through the door of her eldest brother's office.

As the leader of the Sutton clan, he oversaw the daily operations of The Sinner's Palace. But they each had their part in the running of their small empire. And she was about to remind him of hers.

Her brother's head was lowered, and he was poring over something on his desk when she stalked toward him.

"Caro," he greeted when he looked up, rising to his feet from behind his desk with the massive, carved lion legs. "How is our forgetful patient?"

"I cannot keep the truth from him for much longer, Jasper," she blurted. "It is unfair, not just to Gavin, but to me as well."

Jasper quirked a dark brow and stroked his jaw. "*Gavin* is he? That is just a bit too familiar, do you not think, sister?"

His unspoken words were heavy between them. Considering what had happened with Philip, he may as well have said. She was glad he had not, for it did not require her to discuss that spineless horse's arse. Bad enough he had almost deceived her into marrying him; her discovery that he had been bedding one of the ladybirds at The Sinner's Palace was a pain she had no wish to revisit.

Caro was more than happy to turn her attention toward the far more important matter at hand. "Gavin is his name. The name we are keeping from him, just as we keep him from his family each day."

"Ever the warrior, Caro." Her brother shook his head. "You must trust me. We're keeping his name a secret from him for good reason."

"Aye, *your* good reason," she spat. "But not his. How can you be so selfish, Jasper? So heartless? What good does this do him? What good does it do anyone to perpetuate a lie?"

Her voice was shrill as she ended on the last question, and that was likely in part because of her overburdened emotions. It had been months since Philip had dashed her heart to jagged bits, but she had yet to recover fully. Having a patient to look after had been the distraction and the sense of usefulness she had needed. But when Jasper had recognized Gavin and then promptly forced her into secrecy, the distraction had been ruined. Her loyalty to her brother was stronger than her devotion to a stranger, and Jasper knew it. He had preyed upon it, in fact.

Her brother stalked around his desk instead of immediately answering, and went to a sideboard where he poured two glasses of gin.

He turned toward her, holding a glass out as if it were a peace offering. "Calm yourself, sister. Some drops of jackey to ward off the sting of your conscience? Works a charm, I'm given to understand, for those who still possess one."

"I don't want your cursed spirits," she said, refusing to accept the glass. "Pour it down your own gullet."

"Suit yourself, Caro." He tossed back the liquid in first one glass, then the other. "Your loss."

"It is morning," she pointed out acidly.

"Never a better time to indulge," he said, unrepentant. "That tasted like another."

She was sure Jasper was needling her as a means of distraction, but Caro was not pleased.

"Our father was a souse," she called to his retreating back.

Jasper did not pause his stride. At the sideboard, he filled both glasses once more, before turning back to her. "I ain't a souse. Merely a brother who doesn't want to listen to your nonsense. Our guest can't recall a bleeding thing. He's safest where he is. Christ, you're the one who stitched him together again. You ought to know better than anyone that whoever attacked him wanted 'im to cock up his toes. It's best if the bastards believe he did."

She watched as her brother drained the replenished glasses, wincing on the last. "It is best for whom, however? Do you not think the Winters capable of protecting him? And do you not think he would be well-pleased to be among his people, to know who he is?"

Her brother crossed his booted feet at the ankles, leaning against the sideboard, pinning her with a glare. "No, I don't think, Caroline. Else I would have returned 'im to the bloody Winters the moment I recognized 'is mangled carcass."

Caroline.

Her brother's use of her full given name rang like a reproach between them, more surely than his tone of voice. Every Sutton had a shortened name except Jasper. But that was to be expected, for he was their leader. And as Rafe had once pointed out, *what the devil shall we call him, Ass?* Everyone had guffawed except Jasper, who had scowled and threatened to cut off his brother's ballocks and feed them to his dogs.

In this moment, Caro did not think such a sobriquet would be wrong.

She planted her hands on her hips and glared at him. "And why should he not go to his family? If someone had found Logan and kept him from us in the same way, how would you feel?"

Shadows passed over her brother's countenance. Without answering, he presented her with his back and filled the glasses a third time.

"Jasper." She moved toward him, loving her brother, hating to see him filled with such torment, for it was the same pain that had been plaguing her ever since their brother had gone. "I know you miss him. Pray, think of how wrong this is. Think of Loge out there somewhere, hurt as badly as Gavin Winter, or worse. Think of someone keeping him from us—"

Her brother spun back to face her with such haste, the gin splashed over his hands. "He is bloody well *dead*, Caro. Gone to Rothisbone. Thinking about Loge out there somewhere would be for naught. He ain't out there. He's gone. This is different. Gavin Winter is a separate matter entirely, and I'll thank you to trust me to 'andle it."

Tears bit at her eyes at the vehemence of Jasper's response, the sharpness in his voice. He had just spoken aloud the words none of them had been willing to say, to openly acknowledge.

"You do not know for certain that Loge is dead," she countered, swallowing down a lump of emotion—sadness, fear, she knew not what. "He could still be alive. The Winters are likely fearing the worst about Gavin. He has been here with us for almost a fortnight, with no word. Would you truly wish the agony we have experienced upon others?"

"It isn't your affair," her brother said, and then he drained the glasses he held in quick succession.

She had known that Logan's disappearance had taken a toll upon them all, but Jasper had seemed to take it especially hard. Almost as if he felt responsible for what had happened. This ruthlessness he was exhibiting now, extraordinary even by his previous, dubious standards, troubled her.

"But it is my concern," she argued quietly, worried for her brother. "You have made it so by forcing me to continue to lie to Gavin, to pretend I do not know who he is and that I am keeping his presence here a secret from my family. He wants to speak with you, to explain himself, and he is capable of walking about on his own strength now. We cannot keep him forever trapped in a room. What shall we do when he heals completely?"

Wisely, she refrained from mentioning that he had been walking about naked when she had entered his chamber. Jasper's mood was volatile enough without such an inflammatory revelation.

"You let me worry about that when the time comes," her brother said, stern and commanding. "We are Suttons, Caro. Our loyalty to each other is first. Always. Do not forget you promised me you would allow me to 'andle this."

She clenched her jaw, knowing there was nothing more she could do for now. When the walls came down inside Jasper, there was no more talking, no more bargaining. He had decided, and that was that. And he was not wrong. She *had* made him that promise.

She would concede this battle with him.

But not the war.

Caro nodded. "As you wish it, brother. I will leave you to your work. But please, I beg you, no more spirits this morning."

"It's as it *must* be, Caro. Never doubt that."

But as she left her brother's office, the doubt was rife and heavy upon her, weighing her down more than ever. She was not going to surrender. Gavin Winter deserved better.

* * *

He knew he did not deserve the glory which had been delivered to the chamber. But he was going to accept it, just the same.

A tub.

A true bath.

Finally, he could be clean.

So many days in his sickbed, followed by making use of the bowl and pitcher when he had regained his strength enough to make a rough attempt at removing the stink from himself. It had rendered him desperate for clean, warm water surrounding him. Randall and one of the other hell guards had hauled the tub upstairs and filled it.

After his disastrous attempt at dressing the day before, he was ready to begin anew. He could not wait to get inside and wash away the stench of his illness, which he could not help but to feel had been haunting him. *Hell*, for as long as he lived, he would still recall the scent of the ointment Caro had applied to his wound, and that was to say nothing of the acrid sharpness of his own sweat.

Little wonder he had sent Caro running from the chamber, never to return. Not only had he been naked before her, but he was also a hulking, stinking beast. When he had been abed, he had not realized the full extent of his size and height.

Yesterday, as he had been testing his ability to amble about the chamber, and when she had come rushing to his aid following the spell of dizziness… Well, it had occurred to him afterward that he was a rather large chap. His fists alone were massive, and he could not seem to shake the aches in them, the feeling of them pounding against something.

He sighed and slowly, painstakingly, lowered himself into the bath. His limbs were stiff from lack of use. His wound still pained him, but for the first time, surrounded by the heated, clean water, he felt as if he were well and truly alive. It was a glorious feeling.

So damned glorious that when a knock sounded on his door, he called for the person to enter without having a second thought about what had unfolded the day before. Without supposing it may be Caro on the other end of the portal.

The door creaked open. A face appeared in the crack, and hazel eyes settled upon him, searing him to his soul.

Damnation, she was a gorgeous woman.

"Caro." He attempted to brace his arms on the tub so he could slide lower beneath the water, but when he moved his wounded arm, pain sank its jaws into him, biting hard. Though he did his best to muffle the oath, the curse that fled his tongue was blistering.

He needn't have worried that he had offended her, however. Caro came charging into the room, the door closing at her back.

"You must take care, or you will injure yourself further when you are just beginning to heal," she warned, her tone reminiscent of someone else's he knew.

At least, he thought it was. The murky mists of his mind were stubborn in their persistent refusal to relinquish his secrets. Oh, how he wished he could remember even the tiniest speck of his past. Anything at all. Still, there was something about a stern reckoning that made him think he had heard it before. Not from Caro Sutton, but from another woman who was dear to him.

A mother?

Surely not a wife?

He did not want to think his heart belonged to another. But the hell of it was, he had no notion. Not the slightest shred of an inkling. Every memory he had once possessed had turned to dust.

"Have you nothing to say for yourself, sir?" Caro asked, averting her gaze as she bustled past him with a tray of more mixtures and elixirs.

If he had to guess, he would say it was yet another of her healing unguents. Each day, it seemed, she brought him a new salve, ointment, poultice, tea. She was forever trying to heal him.

And she was also turning to face him, pinning him with a ferocious glare now, awaiting his response, he supposed.

He found his voice at last. Rough and husky, partially from the desire that simmered in his veins whenever she was in the vicinity, even when he was doused in pain. But there, nonetheless.

"Forgive me, Caro?"

Her dark brow rose. "For?"

"Causing your displeasure." Indeed, if there was anything he wanted—even more than regaining his memory—it was her pleasure.

In every way. Pity he was in no condition to offer her that just now. And hell, he did not know if he was a skilled lover. He would most certainly like to believe it.

She pursed her lips, her fingers burrowing into the skirt of her gown and twisting. "You do not cause me displeasure. The lack of care you take with yourself, however, does. You must remember the severity of your injuries. Your movements with the wounded arm need to be slow and measured. No pulling at the stitches, or you will ruin my work before you are properly healed and I can remove them."

"Slow and measured," he repeated, trying to ignore the

sudden rising of his cock below the water. "Of course. I'll do better, I will."

They frowned at each other as his words fell between them.

She nodded. "You must, for your own sake."

"Not a gentleman, am I?" he wondered aloud.

Her lips parted, and for a moment, he thought he read something in her eyes before she blinked, banishing it. And then he supposed he must have been imagining the entire affair.

"You are indeed a gentleman," she countered. "At least you are not walking about, bold as you please today, bare-arsed as a babe."

She sent him a gentle, teasing smile to blunt the sting of her words.

"You should not be here," he told her, thinking it must be wrong for an unwed lady to be alone with him thus. Surely her brothers would skin him alive if they were to learn of the familiarity he had with their beautiful sister. "It was not my intention to—"

"Oh, hush," she interrupted. "You are an invalid. I know you haven't any secret desire to seduce me."

She smiled at him, and all he could think about was how very wrong she was, and how mayhap he *was* a bad man. A scandalous rogue. An incorrigible scoundrel. An out and out rakehell. Because he *did* want to seduce her. Since he'd grown well enough to manage a cockstand, he had lain awake at night thinking of little else.

"What if I were to say I do?" he asked, feeling bold.

And stupid.

Likely, it was the warmth of the water. The abating of the pain in his arm now that he was holding still. Or mayhap it was just her eyes, trapping him. She was the loveliest woman he had ever seen. *Hell*—since he had arisen from the abyss, she had been the *only* woman he had seen, but he understood instinctively he had not known one who affected him in the same manner. She was uncommonly warm and caring, and he understood that instinctively as well.

Caro Sutton took his breath and made his heart beat fast.

"What if you were to say you have a secret desire to seduce me?" she echoed, color tingeing her cheekbones as she repeated the question.

He wished he had more strength. He wished he knew his bloody name.

"Aye," he told her. "What if I were to say that?"

Her lips parted. Full, tempting, pink lips. Riper than a summer berry. Had he ever *eaten* a summer berry? If he had, he could not recall.

"I would tell you that you are bound to be disappointed," she told him primly, dashing his hopes. "I do not allow my patients to be so bold."

"Patients?" Now that was intriguing. He had taken note that Caro was a deft hand when it came to tending to a man on his sickbed. But now he realized how little he knew of her. How little they had spoken since he had been well enough to engage in conversation. "Have you many others then, Miss Sutton?"

He did not like the notion. It made his gut clench. Somehow, over the course of his sojourn to regain his strength, he had become enamored of her. He had come to think of her as *his*. However, there was a world beyond this chamber of hers, though it was one he would not recognize. He would do best to remember that.

"You are my only patient at the moment," she said softly, seeming to relent. Her gaze dipped to the water and then moved away with haste. "However, I am the healer here at The Sinner's Palace. You are by no means the first to whom I have tended."

Of course he would not be. She was far too skilled for him to be her first patient.

He studied her, noting she looked as if she wanted to run. "You needn't stay here with me. I promise I ain't going to drown."

As the words left him, he frowned. For there it was again in the imperfection of his speech, the hint that he was not a gentleman at all. Frustration rose, along with impatience. He had hoped his loss of memory would have been temporary—the result of the blows he had taken to the head. But it had been some time since he had initially been attacked. Far too long…

"You had better not drown, sir," she said crisply, still wringing her fingers in the drapery of her serviceable gown. It was an uninteresting shade of gray, but even the unattractiveness of her dress did nothing to detract from her allure. "I have fought quite hard to make certain you survive."

"And I am grateful to you for your efforts," he returned, meaning those words. "I am a stranger, and you have been going to great lengths to protect me. I worry about the burden I am to you. Even this bath must attract some notice in your household, no?"

Her lips thinned, and her shoulders stiffened. But then she smiled that radiant smile of hers, and he forgot all about her initial reaction. Forgetting came deuced easy to him these days.

"You must not fret over me." She turned away, hastening to the tray she had brought and fussing with the contents once more. There was the distinctive sound of an upending vial. "Damn it all."

He had made her uncomfortable, he supposed. But he was not certain if his gratitude or his nudity were the cause. Mayhap both.

"I do fret over you, Caro," he said, wishing he were not

naked in the bath just now, despite the pleasant warmth of the water licking at his skin. "You are far too good to me. I do not deserve any of the risks you have taken on my behalf, nor all the time you have spent making certain I healed properly. I owe you a great deal."

His very life, in fact.

"You do not." If possible, her shoulders stiffened even more as she rushed to mop up her spill, back still turned toward him.

There was an edge in her voice he could neither define nor understand.

She knocked over another item on the tray and cursed again.

"I owe you my life," he dared to counter before hurrying to add more. "You needn't linger here if it makes you uncomfortable, Caro. If *I* make you uncomfortable."

She turned back to him in a swirl of skirts, eyes wide. "Of course you do not. Forgive me. I am being a wretch."

He was sure she could never be one.

"You are not yourself today," he observed. "I assumed it was because of me."

Because he was naked in his bath, and he was saying things which he ought not.

She shook her head. "Of course not. I came to make certain you had everything you needed for your bath, and I arrived too late. I meant to come before you were in the water and…bereft of garments."

Then her flustered state was down to his nudity. And she was attracted to him, as he was to her.

Thank all the angels and the saints and…anyone he could not recall, too.

"Fancy way of saying naked," he observed.

Her flush returned, but her gaze never wavered from his. "Yes. It is." She cleared her throat. "I should leave you to your bath. If you need anything, Randall will bring you some food and tea in the next hour."

With that warning, she fled from the chamber.

He watched her go, disappointment unfurling, along with another feeling he was more than familiar with. Just as it had every day since he had opened his eyes to find himself a guest at The Sinner's Palace with nary a hint of memory, frustration hit him with the force of a blow.

CHAPTER 3

"You and Jasper are keeping a secret from the rest of us."

At the unexpected voice behind her, Caro jumped, spilling the mixture she had been creating all over her work table.

"Blast!" The oath fled her lips before she could contain it, for she had spent days attempting various combinations of ingredients, testing and trying until she achieved a mixture which pleased her.

A mixture that was now dripping to the damned floor instead of helping Gavin's wound when she removed his stitches, as had been her intention. Worse, she had not yet written down the measurements and ingredients so that she could recreate it. She had been rushing and had not taken care to copy down her efforts.

How she regretted that carelessness now.

Caro spun around to find her sister Penelope watching her, hands on her hips.

"Pen, you gave me a fright, and now my ointment is all

over the bloody ground," Caro snapped. "Could you not have given me a warning?"

"I knocked. You were talking to yourself. Something about camphor and unguents, unless I'm mistaken." Pen raised a brow, distinctly unapologetic. "But I have no doubt you will make another. Tell me, what is happening? You and our eldest brother have been conspiring like a pair of Seven Dials footpads, and I don't bloody well like it."

Caro and Pen were close in age, and they had been as inseparable as twins for much of their lives. However, in recent years, she and Pen had grown somewhat apart as her sister's interest in the darker parts of their world distracted her. Especially her interest in one wastrel, rakehell lord. Caro did not approve of him. Pen did.

And, well, they had naturally butted heads, both being stubborn Suttons. The distance between them had grown. Caro had thrown herself into her role as the Sutton healer. So it was that she did not feel obligated to tell Pen the truth about Gavin Winter, beyond the fact that Jasper had made her vow not to tell anyone else. Besides, she feared Pen would go running to her no-account friend Lord Aidan with the tale. For if ever there had been someone one could not trust with damning information, it was he.

"Nothing is happening," Caro deflected calmly, "except that my sister is intruding upon my work and making me spill my efforts before they can be of any use. All because she seems to think I am keeping a secret from her."

But Pen was undeterred, her eyes narrowing. "I *think* you are keeping a secret because you *are*."

Caro eyed her sister across the tiny room beside the kitchens of The Sinner's Palace, the lone space she had claimed for her healing efforts. Nothing but bare walls, a table, and all her herbs and instruments and vials and jars. Better than no place at all, she reminded herself.

"You may think whatever you like, Pen, but that will not bring my ointment back to me. It is quite ruined."

Indeed, a glance to the floor proved it had slid down her gown, leaving a wet stain in its wake, only to fall upon her slipper before landing on the floor in a worthless lump. She had spent days perfecting this version of the healing ointment she applied to her brothers' cuts and wounds whenever they were involved in fights. And she had been so certain she had been close to developing a final combination of ingredients that would enable wounds to heal faster and with less pain, all while minimizing contagion.

Gone now.

"I understand how important your salves and whatnots are to you," Pen said, her tone softening, "and you must know I would never wish to make you spill them. However, I *do* want you to tell me the truth. Why are you and Jasper whispering and spending so much time together? The two of you are ordinarily at odds, spitting fire and throwing blades at each other."

Caro sighed. It was true that she and Jasper often disagreed. The matter of Gavin Winter was not unlike any of the other occasions upon which they had found themselves at odds. It was also true that she was a healer, and that referring to her creations as *salves and whatnot* was an insult.

She decided to keep her attention firmly pinned upon the latter rather than addressing her sister's other concerns. "Do you have any inkling how much time I spend reading and experimenting during the creation of my salves and whatnots?"

Pen rolled her eyes heavenward. "Why do I suspect you're about to tell me?"

The truth was, not even Caro knew how much time she spent upon being the Sutton healer. But it was easily half of each day, if not most of the day.

Caro reached for a freshly laundered rag and bent to clean the remnants of her ointment from the scarred floorboards. "You needn't mock. We cannot all go gadding about with disreputable rogues. Some of us must tend the flock."

If there was bitterness in her voice, it was not because she did not enjoy being the Sutton healer. On the contrary, she loved tending to all who needed her efforts. She enjoyed reading, expanding her knowledge, and experimenting. Her dream of being a physician would never come to fruition, for she had been born a woman. At least she was able to pursue her calling within the walls of The Sinner's Palace, if nowhere else. However, she could not deny that part of her had come to resent Pen for having no responsibilities at the hell beyond keeping the ledgers, a role which enabled her endless time to run off with Lord Aidan.

"Aidan is not disreputable," Pen denied, her shoulders going back in defiance, chin tilting up. "He is the son of a duke."

"Third son," Caro reminded. "And a despicable wastrel."

"He is a fine gentleman."

Ha! Lord Aidan Weir was neither fine nor a gentleman. Caro snorted as she sought a clean part of the cloth and wiped the fallen ointment from her slipper.

"Of course you would defend him, Pen."

"He needs no defense."

Yet, there was an edge to her sister's voice. A note of desperation, as if Pen herself knew how much of a scandalous rascal the man she had befriended truly was. Whoring, drinking, gambling, and getting Pen into no end of scrapes—the man was not a Sutton favorite, aside from his endless purse and his desire to spend it exclusively at The Sinner's Palace. Caro had always suspected there was something more between her sister and Lord Aidan, but Pen claimed they were friends and nothing more.

"He needs an entire infantry brigade of defense," Caro challenged her sister, straightening once more, a sense of defeat settling over her.

The ointment had numbed her skin, which had been the effect she had been attempting to achieve as a means of aiding the pain a wound caused. But she had no notion of how to recreate her unguent without the precise measurements, and the surprise arrival of her sister and subsequent barrage of questions had stricken those from her mind. She would have to begin anew.

"Why are we speaking of Aidan when you and Jasper are keeping a secret from the family?" Pen demanded, crossing the chamber until she crowded Caro with her presence and her displeasure both. "Tell me what is afoot with you and our eldest brother, and tell me now."

"I have already told you," Caro said, avoiding her sister's gaze, "and it is nothing. No reason. If Jasper and I were speaking, it was a matter regarding The Sinner's Palace and nothing more."

That was true, indirectly.

"Randall has been going to your room a great deal," Pen said. "Are you bedding him?"

Randall? The man was akin to another brother. Moreover, Jasper and their other brothers would have given the poor man a drubbing and then sacked him. Although Caro and her sisters were not unfamiliar with the seedier matters of life—thanks to living in a gaming hell—the Suttons made certain they were protected.

Caro shook her head. "Of course I am not bedding Randall. Our brothers would never allow it. Are you bedding Lord Aidan?"

Pen scowled. "Of course not. We are *friends*, Caro."

Caro did not bother to point out the most unusual nature of such a friendship between a girl from the rookeries and the third son of a duke who was known for his wild ways.

She shrugged, then returned to the task of cleaning her work table. "I suppose I shall have to accept your word on the matter, just as you shall have to accept mine."

* * *

HE WAS GROWING IMPATIENT. The four walls surrounding him were cruel mockeries. This morning, he had risen and dressed on his own. He had eaten the hearty meal Randall had brought him. He had waited for Caro to appear.

And he was still waiting.

Pacing did nothing to take the edge off the irritation rising within him. He had regained his strength. The time had come to emerge from this bloody room. But because of his indebtedness to Caro, he would not leave without first making her aware of his decision.

He needed to face her siblings. He did not cower and hide. He faced his demons.

At least, he instinctively felt as if he did. The hell of it was, he did not know. And the longer he remained trapped in this room, the more damning the emptiness in his mind became. After he had first arisen and his mind had been lucid enough to understand that he had lost all memories of the man he had been, he had hoped that in time, a few days, with some rest, all would return to him.

But that had not happened.

A knock sounded at the door.

Fucking finally.

"Enter," he called, stalking across the chamber, feeling much like a cat about to pounce on a bird.

And there she was at last, with wisps of auburn curls

framing her face, her hazel eyes wide as she took in the sight of him, a beast who had been too long kept in his cage.

"You've dressed," she announced as the door closed at her back.

He inclined his head, itching to sweep past her and cross the threshold into whatever world awaited beyond. "Aye."

She was bearing a tray once more, he noted, and it was laden with more pots and vials and instruments. He stepped forward and took it from her, using only his uninjured arm.

"You mustn't," she protested, trying to wrest the tray back from him, "you'll hurt yourself."

"I'm strong," he protested, proving the truth of his words as he pulled the tray from her grasp with ease. "I'm not an invalid any longer, Caro. It's time for me to get out of this bloody room."

Demonstrating further veracity, he easily walked with the tray and deposited it upon the bedside table.

"I need to remove the stitches from your wound," she said, following him.

He turned back to her, drinking her in. She was such a diminutive thing, and he had not realized it entirely until now, with his strength regained and her standing before him near enough to touch.

Touch.

Suddenly, he could not control the need to experience the softness of her skin beneath his fingertips. A wisp of a curl had fallen on her cheek. Her fresh scent hit him, lush and fragrant in stark contrast to the closed-up chamber before her arrival.

He reached out, gently tracing the curl with the tip of his forefinger first. She held still, her eyes pinned to him. So much gray, a hint of green, and golden-brown in her gaze. He did not think he had ever seen eyes so distinctive on a woman, but he supposed he would have no notion of whether or not he had.

"You are disheveled," he observed.

She caught the plump fullness of her lower lip in her teeth and studied him for what felt like a dozen heartbeats but must have only been one. "I am certain I must look a fright. I was in my work room, attempting to perfect the unguent for your wound."

He was clumsy at this. Had he been a charming man before the knock he'd taken to the knowledge box? A rogue who could charm ladies with ease? He somehow doubted it. Here was a slip of a woman, lovely and so much smaller than he, and yet, she intimidated him. He felt as if he were surrounded by darkness, grasping at slivers of light, but each time he reached, the light slid from his grasp.

"You could never look a fright," he managed to say, still touching that lone curl.

It was silken, exquisite.

What would her cheek feel like? Smooth and soft, like the finest velvet? Caro could seduce a man without trying. She was wearing a pale muslin gown today that was simple enough in construction, with a modest bodice. And yet, she was so damned gorgeous, he ached just looking at her.

His cock rose in his trousers with renewed determination.

Not now, you devil.

"You are being too kind," she said, then bit her lip once more.

Such sweet torture, watching her mouth. Wanting it beneath his. Wanting more than this tiny moment of intimacy between them, yet not knowing how to have it. Not knowing if he *could* have it.

He cleared his throat, trying to chase some of his

conflicting feelings away. "I ain't certain I'm a kind chap. I could be a monster."

Sweet Jesus, what if he was? For some reason, the worry had never occurred to him until now. He stared at his hand, so near to her pale cheek, so large and strong, and suddenly from the murk of his memory surged remembrance. He recalled swinging his fist, the crunch of bone, the bite in his knuckles. He knew the way it felt to hit a man, he thought.

The realization was enough to make him drop his hand away.

"Are you feeling ill?" she asked, worry furrowing her brow. "You've gone pale."

"I...am well." He struggled to make sense of the dark and jagged pieces of his mind. "I may have had a memory return just now, but I...I don't know."

"A memory?" Her brows rose, her voice infused with hope. "What sort of memory?"

He did not want to admit the truth to her, but neither did he want to lie. "Hitting someone. Forming a fist, swinging a punch. I remember how it felt, I think."

Unless he was deluding himself? He'd had many dreams over the course of the past few days as well, but it was impossible to determine what was real, if anything, and what was merely his slumbering mind's madness or attempts to create a history for himself to fill the hollow.

"You remember punching someone?" she repeated, voice hushed, as if she had entered a church and was afraid to speak too loudly.

"Hell." He ran his right hand over his mostly healed face, confusion settling in, battling the desire that blanketed him whenever Caro entered the room. "For a moment, it seemed real, as if it were something I'd done. But now, I don't know."

She was watching him with a stricken expression, those

beautiful eyes of hers wider than ever. "Were you remembering the day you were attacked, do you suppose?"

"Mayhap." A dull ache thumped to life in his head, almost as if to remind him he was working himself too hard. "It doesn't matter, does it? Not if I can't recall the rest."

This time, it was she who touched him, her small, work-reddened hand brushing over his arm in a tender caress. "You will remember. Have faith. You mustn't force yourself. It will return to you in time."

But that was the devil of it. *Would* his memory return?

Frustration rose within him, and he wanted to shrug away from her gentle concern. But he also never wanted her to take her hand away. He wanted the brand of Caro upon him forever, to wear like a shirt.

"I may never remember," he said, trying to keep the fear accompanying that undeniable fact at bay.

And failing.

He gave himself away by trembling. She felt it. He knew she did.

The worry on her countenance tucked itself into his heart. And he wanted to wear her sweet apprehension, her caring, there too. To keep it always, this closeness they had in the cozy confines of her room, when the vastness of the world beyond had yet to reach him. As much as he wanted to leave this chamber, he also recognized it as a haven in that moment.

"You will remember," she repeated, as if he would by her decree.

Her hand was still on his arm. He moved subtly, withdrawing until their bare palms pressed together. His fingers laced through hers.

"I need to leave this room, Caro," he said softly. "I need to speak to your brothers. To earn my keep here if they will have me. I'll not be your burden any longer, nor will I keep you from your bed."

Her fingers tightened on his, concern furrowing her brow. "You cannot. You are still healing."

"I'm healed."

Except for my empty goddamn head.

"I need to remove your stitches," she pointed out.

"Do it now."

"But—"

"Please," he interrupted, entreating her as best as he could. "I can't stay here like this, like a lion in the cage at the Royal Menagerie."

"Have you visited the menagerie?" she asked.

He blinked, sifting through his mind for the answer, and finding none. "I don't know."

Her thumb traveled over his inner wrist in a caress that sent new heat snaking to his groin. "Come and sit by the hearth. I'll remove your stitches."

Damn, he wished the invitation she was offering him was a different one entirely. But he nodded, because his head was aching and because he needed the blasted stitches gone.

And he needed to leave this infernal room.

CHAPTER 4

In the sanctity of her work room, Caro exhaled a deep, shaking sigh of relief. One day had passed since Gavin had confronted her with his need to flee her chamber and face her brothers. But whilst she had removed his stitches and applied an unguent to his still-healing wound, she had persuaded him to wait another day. The salve she had applied to his wound had not been the same as what she had spilled all over the floor the day before, but it had sufficed.

Her guilt, however…

That was gnawing at her steadily, like an attic mouse chewing up everything it could find.

She had attempted to speak with Jasper this morning before breakfast to persuade him that Gavin needed to emerge from the room and at least be permitted to go about the private quarters of The Sinner's Palace. However, her brother had been in bed.

The muffled female giggles traveling to Caro through his chamber door—belonging to no less than two different women, unless she was mistaken—had proven a strong deterrent. As had her brother's half-hearted urging to return in three hours.

Jasper had once fancied himself smitten with Genevieve Winter, the sole female in the Winter family. But as the Winters were sworn enemies—and the greatest competition—to the Suttons, his attempts at wooing had not gone well. Ever since Genevieve Winter had refused his suit, Jasper had been bedding every lightskirt in the East End, or so it seemed.

There was nothing for her to do this morning save spend the next few hours of solitude working on her medical stores. Unguents and tonics were always in need. And as Caro's hands went to work, she tried to turn her mind away from thoughts of the handsome stranger who didn't know his name. The man she had come to know and care for during his impromptu stay at The Sinner's Palace.

She was fortunate enough to have her small garden of herbs which she could tend and harvest to aid in her endeavors. Fortunate she had this room, where she was free to work on the experiments most important to her. Fortunate for the shelf of highly prized—and dear—books stacked on the corner of her work table.

There was much to concern herself with outside of the troubling matter of Gavin Winter. Beyond his vibrant-green eyes and dark, tousled hair, his towering height, decadent muscles, handsome face, and slashing cheekbones and jaw. Beyond that beautiful mouth, those big hands that touched her with such tenderness. Beyond the confusion in his eyes, the desperation edging his deep voice.

No. You must not think of him, Caro. There is naught you can do for now. Concentrate on your work, girl.

She forced herself to tamp down the longing rising within her, telling herself it was foolishness. Perhaps something wrought by the length of time she had been tending to

Gavin, which was longer than she had ever nursed another. Moreover, he was not one of her brothers, nor one of the guards she considered in the same vein.

She turned her attention to her remaining stores, which were growing thin. Her ability to grow her own herbs only took her so far. She inevitably needed to replenish them and other items at the apothecary. Taking up her quill, she set her pen to the paper awaiting her on her table and began to make a list of supplies she would need to purchase soon.

Purslain for coughs.

Chamomile oil to relieve swelling and other pains.

Ointment of yarrow for wounds.

Lavender and oil of spike.

Horehound, fennel, asparagus.

"Caro."

The voice, deep and familiar, and so very unexpected, made her shriek and upend her inkwell.

"Forgive me. I didn't mean to startle you," he said.

As she frantically took up one of her laundered rags and attempted to blot up the stain growing over her list, he was suddenly nearer than ever. His heat and strength burned into her back as his massive hand covered hers.

"Allow me to clean this mess. 'Tis of my own making."

She was frozen. Frozen with a combination of awareness at his nearness, his hand atop hers, his touch making her weak. And too, the knowledge that he had emerged from her room. That he had wandered about The Sinner's Palace on his own, where he could have been recognized. That Jasper would be furious when he discovered what had happened.

To the devil with Jasper.

She licked her suddenly dry lips. "I will clean it. I am at fault for my clumsiness. You needn't fret."

"I am sorry for giving you a fright." His tone was wry, his

voice in her ear, so close that his hot breath skimmed over her flesh, sending a shiver of pure need down her spine.

She turned her head, meeting his gaze. "You are meant to be resting, sir. Abed."

His fingers tightened over hers, and he gave her the most beautiful smile she had ever beheld on a man's lips. "Ah, but being abed and alone is one of the true curses of this life. I could not remain there another moment."

Abed and alone.

For some foolish, wild reason, she thought of joining him there. Of touching him freely and not merely with the intent to soothe, comfort, or heal. Of pressing her mouth to his. Of shedding her clothes and lying with him.

Shocking.

Sinful.

Wrong.

Delicious.

Tempting.

Dangerous.

He was staring at her, waiting, and she realized he had spoken last, but her foolish mind had been too preoccupied with listing words to describe this moment, this man. Oh, why had she been the one to find him, the one to heal him, the one to deceive him?

"You should not be here," she said at last, hating herself for the breathlessness in her tone.

"Here feels like a deuced fine place to be."

They stared at each other, the heat between them rising, a lone spark turning into a raging fire. The devil of it was, here felt like an awfully fine place to be for Caro as well.

She swallowed against a fervent rush of longing. "How did you find me?"

"I followed you."

His confession took her by surprise. He was wilier than

she had supposed, even without his memory. A formidable opponent, she had no doubt. And a man she had been lying to from the moment his eyes had fluttered open, confused and bloodshot.

"This morning?" she asked, trying to decipher when he had begun trailing her about The Sinner's Palace.

Her stops had been many.

"You passed my door, and I followed. You went to the kitchens and emerged with a honey cake."

So she had. Her eyes narrowed. "You have been following me for the entire morning?"

He cocked his head, studying her, hand still on hers, the touch strangely comforting. "I suppose I have been. You flit about like a butterfly, you do. Never staying in one place for long, flying just out of reach, and bright and beautiful."

He thought her bright and beautiful?

Her breath caught. "I am not out of reach now."

"No." He was unsmiling, his gaze intent. "You aren't."

Duty and obligation warred with the desire burning to life within her. She knew she needed to persuade him to go back from whence he had come until she could speak with Jasper. That she should not enjoy his nearness, his touch. That she should be mopping up the spilled ink. And yet, she didn't want to do anything she was supposed to just now.

Loyalty was a cold comfort. Still, she was a Sutton before she was anything else. And keeping Gavin a secret was important for his safety. Someone wanted him dead, she reminded herself.

She mustered up a protest. "You should return to your chamber—"

The rest of her words were stifled beneath his lips. His lips on hers. His mouth moved. It was warm, supple. He was kissing her. Lord in heaven, Gavin Winter was *kissing* her, and it was...

Wondrous.

She forgot about the ink which had been spilled. His hand left hers, his good arm sliding around her waist. She settled her palms on his shoulders, so large, radiating strength and reassurance. He smelled of shaving soap and clean linen, and no scent had ever been more inviting.

Caro had kissed before. But she had never been kissed quite like *this* before. Gavin Winter's lips on hers… *Oh*, she could not find the words to describe it.

Her mind was racing, tumbling over itself, her emotions colliding with sensation, reason and doubt and duty crashing together. She should not be kissing him, and she knew it. She was deceiving him. Their families were operating under a tentative truce which would be destroyed when the Winters discovered the Suttons had been keeping their lost brother from them.

Yet, Gavin's lips on hers were smooth and knowing, teasing and gentle, worshipful and masterful all at once. He kissed like an angel and the devil. He tempted and promised. Longing swept over her, so sudden and ferocious she trembled beneath the force of it.

When his big hand splayed over her lower back, drawing her nearer to him, there was no mistaking the disparity between them. He was tall, all sinew and corded muscle, his chest a wall against which her breasts crushed. But there was another part of him that was equally hard. The same part of him she had done her utmost to forget about.

He was thick and long, pressing into her belly with a prominence she could not deny pleased her. Caro knew an aching, tingling, unbearable answering need between her thighs. He traced over the seam in her lips, seeking, and she opened for him. His tongue dipped into her mouth, claiming and yet sweetly tantalizing.

Weakly, she tried to summon some resistance. To remind

herself of the myriad reasons why she should not be kissing this man. Why she should not be holding him close instead of tearing herself away.

But all she could do was feel.

Feel his hand gliding up her spine to caress the nape of her neck. Feel his lips delivering slow, tender kisses to the corners of her mouth. Feel the wet glide of his tongue against hers. Feel the sparks of passion lighting into roaring, uncontrollable flame.

Everything else ceased to matter.

Her heart raced. No kiss had ever been better. Nor had she ever hungered for another as she wanted this man. This man who did not know his name, who had no memories. This man she had found beaten and broken and bloodied in the cobblestones.

Yearning unfurled. He kissed down her throat, and her head fall back of its own accord, giving him more of her skin. Surrendering to the passion blazing so brightly between them.

He kissed his way to her ear. "Sweet Caro."

She became aware of her body in a new way. Her breasts were heavy and full, her nipples hard beneath her stays. Caro could not keep the sigh from fleeing her as he pressed a kiss to her throat, his tongue flicking over her skin.

"You taste as good as you smell," he whispered against her flesh.

The room felt as if it were spinning around them. Everything was a tumult of sensation and color and light. She caressed his shoulders, needing more of him, needing to touch him everywhere.

"Caro?"

Her panic was as sudden as it was acute at the unexpected voice of her sister at the opposite end of the room. She tore herself from Gavin's arms and turned to face Pen, who stood at the threshold of Caro's work room, her expression slack with shock as she took in Gavin.

"Pen," she said quickly, smoothing down her skirts as she sought something to do with her hands.

That was when she realized there was ink upon her fingers, and she had smeared a great deal of it over her gown. In horror, she glanced back at Gavin to see smears of black ink on his coat, cravat, and shirt. Everywhere she had touched him, there was the evidence of her wickedness.

"A Winter?" her sister asked.

More shock hit Caro, for she had not expected Pen to recognize Gavin. And now that she had—if she were to reveal Gavin's identity before him—

"Please go, Pen," she said, imploring her sister with her eyes.

But Pen was undeterred. She remained where she was, her gaze narrowing as it flicked over Gavin with blatant curiosity. "Is he the secret, then? I heard—"

"Get out!" Caro blurted, startling herself with the vehemence in her tone.

But what was she to do? She was conflicted, torn between the promise she had made to her brother and the newfound emotions roiling through her. Gavin Winter's kisses had utterly ruined her. She could scarcely make sense of anything.

Pen blinked. "Caro."

"Please," she entreated, more softly this time.

"Forgive me," Gavin said, flicking a cautious gaze from Caro to Pen, then back to Caro again. "I should not have overstepped."

Yes, she wanted to tell him. *You should have. And you should do it again.*

But she tamped down the unworthy sentiment. Had she learned no lessons at all after Philip? It would seem not.

"Pen, I will find you in a few minutes. If you will excuse us?"

"If I excuse you, are you going to smear more ink on him?" her sister queried with an unrepentant grin.

"Pen, just go."

With a superior lifting of her eyebrows, Pen turned and left the work room, the door clicking closed in the silence that had descended.

With another sigh, Caro faced Gavin, wincing as she took in the manner in which she had mussed him. *Bloody blazes*, she had stained a good portion of his garments and nearly untied his sullied cravat in the process. She had not recalled her fingers working the knot.

"I am sorry, Caro," he said softly, his gaze dipping to her lips, then back. "I should not have kissed you."

For a reason she could not define, the sentiment bothered her. She did not want him to regret their kiss. Although she knew *she* should regret it, and that it must not be repeated, she hated to think she had been alone in the kiss's effect.

"I am sorry as well," she said nonetheless.

"I have no right to kiss you when I do not know who the hell I am," he said, frowning.

Guilt pricked her anew.

Tell him, urged her conscience. *Tell him who he is now. Tell him he is Gavin Winter.*

She wanted to. Heavens, how she wanted to.

But when she opened her mouth to speak, his name did not emerge. "We were caught up in the moment. Think nothing of it."

He nodded slowly, his countenance still unhappy. "Who was that just now?"

It occurred to her that she had not introduced them. Partially because Pen had somehow already known who he was, and partially because she could not offer a name to her sister. She was not ready to discuss Jasper's demand that she keep Gavin's presence at The Sinner's Palace a secret, along with keeping his name from him.

"It was my sister, Pen," she managed. "I must speak to her so that she does not go to our brothers."

That was only a partial falsehood, she reasoned.

Gavin's jaw tensed. "I need to speak to your brothers, Caro. My honor demands it."

She hated the deceptions she was perpetuating. "We will speak to them together when the time is right."

"The time is now. Do you not suppose your sister is already running to them?"

Was Pen? Caro thought it unlikely, though she could not be certain.

"All the more reason for me to seek her out now and for you to return to my room." She studied her handiwork once more, the inky handprints on his chest and shoulders, the smears on the pristine white of his neck cloth. "You need to change before you confront anyone, I am afraid."

He glanced down at the ink and cursed.

"Wait for me here," she said. "I will speak with my sister and return."

* * *

"You were kissing Gavin Winter."

Pen's proclamation made Caro wince and cast a glance around to make certain no one else was within listening distance. "Keep your voice down, Pen."

Her sister raised a brow. "All this time, I thought you were bedding Randall. But you've been keeping Gavin Winter in your room, haven't you?"

She had found her sister in the hall outside the kitchens, waiting for her. But Pen had refused to go elsewhere to speak, and Caro had felt oddly placated by the notion of remaining near to Gavin anyway. Now, she regretted her hasty capitulation.

"Cease saying his name, if you please."

"Does Jasper know you're bedding a Winter?" Pen asked, ignoring her.

"I'm not bedding a Winter." She scowled at her sister. "What you saw was…"

Absolutely exquisite.

The most stunning moments of my life.

No, she must not say any of that.

She cleared her throat, all too aware of the heat rising in her face, giving her away. "What you saw was a mistake, one which shan't be repeated."

Pen crossed her arms over her chest, looking distinctly unimpressed and unconvinced. "You do know it is the talk of the East End, that Gavin Winter is nowhere to be found and he's got a match with Jeremiah Jones."

Caro frowned. "How did you recognize him, and how do you know what match he has next?"

"Lord Aidan," Pen answered. "He took me to one of the matches. Gavin Winter is a ferocious beast of a man. You should have seen him pummeling the poor fellow."

A shudder went through her at the thought of Gavin facing an opponent with his fists. She did not like violence, and she never had. Mayhap that was one of the reasons she had so readily thrown herself into the business of being the Sutton healer. It was her means of making amends for that which was out of her control. The Suttons were a rough and ragged band, it was true.

"He does not know who he is, Pen," she admitted softly. "I found him nearly dead in the streets and had some of the guards take him to my room. Someone tried to kill him."

"He doesn't know who he is? But how can that be?"

"I have been poring over my books, and it is not unheard of for someone who receives a blow or blows to the head to suffer from this affliction," she explained. "Sometimes, the memory returns. Other times, it may not."

She hoped, for Gavin's sake, that his would, even if it meant he would realize the depth of her deception. Even if it meant he would never be able to forgive her for her complicity in the lies her brother had required her to tell.

"He has no notion of anything?" Pen asked.

"All he knows is what I have told him. You were right to think Jasper and I have been keeping a secret, and that Gavin Winter is it. But Jasper does not want Gavin to know who he is just yet. Nor does he want anyone else to know who Gavin is or why he is here."

"Why *is* he here?" Pen prodded. "Why not simply contact the Winters and see him gone?"

Gavin and *gone* in the same sentence made a curious ache pierce Caro's heart. How was it possible she had spent such a short amount of time nursing him back to health, and yet she felt as if she had always known him? Why could she not bear the thought of never seeing him again?

She shook her head, as if so doing, she could dislodge the troublesome thoughts which had taken up residence in her stubborn mind. But that wasn't so. They were there. Gavin Winter was there. So, too, the memory of his lips on hers.

"Jasper has not seen fit to enlighten me." And that still rankled, Caro could not deny it. "He claims he has a purpose but that I must trust him and remember my loyalty is as a Sutton first."

"Aye, and so it is," Pen agreed. "You can trust me, Caro. I'll not tell a soul Gavin Winter is here."

"Stop saying his name," she muttered, for hearing it aloud brought a creeping sense of fear.

Fear that someone would overhear. Fear that whoever it

was who had attacked Gavin and left him for dead would return. But that this time, the monsters would not stop until they succeeded.

"What shall I call him, then?"

What indeed?

"The patient," she suggested.

"The patient," Pen repeated, a skeptical note in her voice.

Frustration bit at her. "Have you a better suggestion?"

Pen sighed. "I suppose not. The patient shall have to do."

"Do not tell Lord Aidan," Caro said next.

"But we tell each other everything. He is my dearest friend."

Bloody damn blazes. If they had to rely upon the honor of Lord Aidan Weir, their ship was as good as at the bottom of the ocean.

"You are a Sutton first," she reminded her sister. "Lord Aidan is not."

Nor was he trustworthy. Or a gentleman. Or anyone in whom her sister should be placing such care and loyalty. But that was a matter for another day. Besides, it was not anything their brothers and their sister Lily had not already warned Pen about.

Pen was stubborn as a mule.

Pen's jaw hardened. "As you wish it. But if he asks, I won't lie, Caro."

"Why would he ask?"

"He is perceptive."

"He is a drunken wastrel who spends all his waking hours gaming and whoring," Caro countered.

"If you are going to be hateful about Aidan, I'll not keep your secret."

Caro glared at her sister. They were at daggers drawn. "Fine. I need you to do this for me, Pen."

Her sister raised a brow. "Then apologize for what you said about my friend."

Caro heaved a sigh and barely resisted rolling her eyes. "I am sorry."

"For?"

"For speaking honestly about Lord Aidan Weir. Henceforth, I will endeavor to lie and tell you he is a paragon of virtue who is selfless, brave, and true."

"Caroline Sutton." Pen scowled.

"Keep my secret and I will not tell Jasper Lord Aidan has been sneaking you into prizefights." It was Caro's turn to raise a brow at her sister. "You must have dressed as a cove to find yourself in the audience."

Pen's scowl faded. "I did, and it was glorious. I regret nothing."

"Pen," she said softly. "I worry about you."

Her sister's chin went up. "You needn't. I do just fine as I am. And I will keep your secret for as long as I am able, Caro."

It was not the promise she wanted, but it was all she was going to wrestle from Pen, and Caro knew it. She inclined her head. "We have a bargain, sister. I won't say a word about your excursions with Lord Aidan, and you will hold your tongue about the patient."

"Aye. I'll hold my tongue about the patient. You just best keep *yours* out of the patient's mouth."

With that, Pen swept past Caro, leaving her standing alone in the corridor, cheeks aflame.

CHAPTER 5

He stood in the small room for what seemed an eternity. The chamber was easily one quarter the size of Caro's room, which had already felt terribly cramped for a man of his size. And for a man who had been kept on one side of the door for far too long.

But here, in this space that was undeniably Caro's territory in a way her chamber was not, he felt even more like a great, lumbering beast. His head nearly scraped the beams of the ceiling. His arms were too long, his fists too large, his shoulders too wide. After attempting to mop up her spilled ink, he had proceeded to knock a tidy pile of books to the floor with his bleeding elbow.

The spine of one of the books had cracked.

He would have to see it restored for her. If indeed he could ever earn the funds to do so or find a goddamn bookbinder. The restrictions of not just his size but his lack of memory weighed heavily upon him in these charged minutes after he had kissed her senseless. His body was still aflame from her response. His attire was yet marked by the ink-stained hands that had caressed him and attempted to undo the pathetic knot he had tied in his cravat.

The cravat felt deuced odd.

He didn't suppose himself the sort of cove who would have often worn one. Seemed too restrictive on his thick neck. Like a noose, ready to choke a man. The darkness of his mind disturbed him. He wondered, once more, who he was. What he had done. Was he a violent man? A criminal, perhaps?

Hell, until he knew, he had no right to touch Caro. No right to kiss her.

Regardless of how much he wanted to, and despite the inconceivable way his mouth on hers had affected him. His cockstand had been rigid and ready, despite the sudden appearance of her sister, which should have been the equivalent of a pail of cold water being poured over his head.

Instead, he was awaiting Caro like a good dog, pacing the length of her little room in five increasingly frustrated strides. Bumping into the bloody table with his hip and emitting a howl of pain. Too big for this room. Too empty-minded to know anything.

Utterly lost and adrift.

He didn't know his name. Didn't know a damned thing about himself. He felt as if he had been a passenger on a ship that had taken on water and sunk to the bottom of the sea, leaving him behind, clinging to the flotsam. And the flotsam was Caro.

He ground his jaw, used his good hand to rake his fingers through his hair, and stalked to the door. Where was she? What was taking so bloody long? And why did she insist upon keeping him from her brothers?

Ignoring the twinge of conscience that told him he had no reason to distrust her, he opened the door slowly, quietly. Caro was down the hall, in heated discussion with her sister.

He heard the same familiar word her sister had uttered upon her earlier disruption.

Winter.

The season of snow and ice.

Why should it feel so familiar? Why should it make an ache begin deep in his gut, as if it called to him in a deeper way? As if he should remember it?

Caro seemed to say something, and he strained to hear it but could not. Then her sister spoke.

What shall I call him, then?

The patient, Caro said.

Guilt hit him. He was eavesdropping upon her, when she had only been an utter angel to him. She had nursed him back to health, had stitched his flesh together, and tended him through infection. Yet how did he repay his beautiful butterfly? By catching her, kissing her, and then distrusting her.

He stepped back, allowing the door to quietly close once more. She was entitled to her privacy. Caro was doing everything in her power to keep him safe. Humility joined the guilt. Who was he, to deserve her concern and consideration?

Who was he at all, damn it?

Would he ever remember?

He returned to pacing this small room, taking greater note of his surroundings for the first time. Initially, Caro had been all he could see. Then, he had been too caught up in a maelstrom of emotions to be observant. However, now, he took note of all the jars, carefully labeled, the neat penmanship. The journal filled with her concise script. Measurements, he noticed, and then he unintentionally slammed his wounded arm into the wall.

Pain seared him, and for a moment he feared he'd torn open his wound anew. But as the discomfort subsided, the door finally opened, revealing a flushed-looking Caro. He rubbed his arm lightly, trying to hide his grimace.

But she had seen it.

Of course she had.

She came rushing to him. "I heard a thump. What is the matter? Have you hurt yourself?"

What a fool he felt. "I am too damned big."

He wondered if he had felt at home in his massive size before. Since everything was new, he could not be sure, but he supposed he would have been accustomed to it, having slowly grown into a larger body over time. However, waking up to find himself a giant was a hell of a realization.

Deuced troubling.

"What do you mean, you are too big?" She frowned as she reached him, her skirts fluttering about her.

"Butterfly," he said again, for she reminded him of one once more.

She blinked, her dark lashes long and luxurious against the paleness of her face. "I beg your pardon?"

He was not making sense. What must she think of him, this great oaf who had appeared in her life as a bloodied carcass? This man she did not know but whose life she had saved.

"You are a butterfly," he elaborated, "and I am a beast. I knocked over your books, and I collided with the wall. That was the thump you heard just now."

"You are not a beast."

"I am, and I will see your book repaired. The spine of one is damaged. It's still intact, but the damage is done. It was an older volume, the leather brittle…"

"You needn't fret over it."

"Yes, I do need to. I should not have broken it. I ought to have been more careful. I should not be here at all, burdening you as I am. Making difficulties for you with your sister, forcing you to keep secrets from the rest of your family. No more, Caro. We must stop this."

The color fled from her, and he realized she thought he was referring to the kisses they had just shared.

"The *secrecy*," he added, emphasizing the word. "I'll not be your cross to bear. I am a man, and whilst I don't know my name, I'll be damned before I cause you any further trouble. You've already done more than I'll ever be able to repay. You saved my life."

She shook her head slowly, shadows he did not understand darkening her eyes. "You are not making difficulties for me. Please, do not worry yourself on my behalf."

"But you were arguing with your sister just now, and over me. Were you not?" he pressed.

She stilled, her gaze searching his. "Were you listening?"

"Aye," he admitted, feeling like the world's greatest arse. "I am sorry for doing it, as I know I should not have."

"What did you hear?" she demanded, a tenseness he could not quite comprehend tingeing her voice.

He wondered at the reason for the change in her demeanor. Was she angry he had been listening? Or was she worrying over what he may have heard? And if so, why? Was there more to his angelic butterfly than a beautiful face and the hands of a healer?

"I heard nothing," he lied, and he was not sure why. Some instinctive prodding within. Perhaps a hint of the man he once had been wearing through the abyss of his empty mind. "You seemed distraught. I continued pacing and broke your book."

She nodded, accepting his deception. "I should look at your arm and make certain you did not reopen the wound so soon after the stitches were removed."

He clenched his jaw at the notion of her touching him after the passionate kisses they had shared. How the hell was he to maintain his composure? To remain unaffected, or at least to pretend that he was?

He swallowed. "Go on, then. Have a peek as you like."

She approached him warily, as if she feared he would take her in his arms and kiss the breath out of her again. And he wanted to. Lord, how he wanted to. But he was a confused jumble of emotions and sensations. Longing, suspicion, desire, and gratitude had all melded into a sick soup within him.

Caro took his coat in a confident grasp and tugged it down his arms. Her seductive scent settled over him once more, and he could not avoid its resulting effect. Damn it, his prick was stirring to awareness again, all from the mere act of shedding his coat.

The shirt she had given him had been modified with additional buttons below the ordinary three at his neckline, enabling him to don the shirt without the pain of having to overexert himself. Caro had thought of everything, and he was bloody thankful for her prescience. For her healing abilities. For her care and concern.

She removed his cravat, but when he attempted to aid in the buttons on his shirt, she chased his fingers. "Allow me."

Well.

He did not think he had ever been undressed by another before. If he had, he certainly possessed no recollection of it. But this, *Caro*, standing in proximity, her small hands brushing over him in quick, efficient movements, her floral perfume coiling around him…it moved him. There was a deeper sense of intimacy involved, mayhap now that they had kissed, but unless he was mistaken, there was something else there. Some nagging sense he was connected to her in a way that went beyond the connection of patient and nurse.

He held still as she pulled the shirt open to reveal his wounded arm. The cool kiss of her fingertips ran over his flesh in a gentle examination that only served to heighten his already painful state of awareness. His breath seemed to freeze, his heart thudding hard and fast in his chest.

"You did not do any further damage, thank heavens," she murmured. "But you must consider your wound as you move about. The skin is newly healed and sensitive. I'll not have you undoing all my efforts."

He made the mistake of looking down at her. Their gazes clashed and held. Her lips parted.

He wanted to kiss her again.

"I promise to take more care," he managed, his voice husky.

"See that you do." Her tone was practical. Almost polite. And yet, she did not move away. Nor did she make any effort to cease touching him.

Her fingers trailed lower, to the skin below his wound. "You have an inking."

He glanced down, watching as her touch traced the letters he had discovered had been etched into his skin. They would not be washed away. "A tattoo," he agreed. "I do not know what it means."

He wished he did. He wished he remembered everything. But then, none of that seemed as important when Caro was near enough to kiss. When Caro was caressing him. He wanted her more than he wanted his next breath.

"It must bear some significance," she said softly. "DDBGD."

"Aye." He knew the letters, had memorized them. Had searched his empty, frustrated mind for any hint as to what they may mean. "I wish I knew."

"Do they represent names, I wonder?" Her gaze lowered, following the progression of her touch as she closed the last D. "Did it hurt?"

She wasn't asking him, she was asking the man he had

once been, and that man was a stranger to him now. The man he had woken up as didn't have the answers. So he said nothing. Instead, he took her hand in his and brought it to his lips for a kiss.

Her swift inhalation was sharp in the quiet of the small room. Her eyes were back on his once more. "I'm sorry for any argument I caused between you and your sister, Caro, but I ain't sorry I kissed you. Are you?"

She swallowed, drawing his attention to the creamy elegance of her throat. "We mustn't do that again."

"Why not?"

Her tongue darted over her lower lip. He stifled a groan.

"It isn't wise," she murmured, tugging her hand free to trail it over his chest.

"Caro." Her name was a growl, leaving him. He caught her wrist, flattening her palm over his heart. "Do you feel that?"

"Yes."

"You make it beat so."

"Oh." She took his hand in hers and guided it over her linen bodice, where her heart was thumping steadily. Quickly. "You do the same to me."

Curse it all, what was it about this woman that made him want to take her up in his arms and keep her there forever? But he knew he could not. He had no right. Moreover, he needed to set some matters straight. He had not forgotten his initial reason for interrupting her here at her work.

"I need to speak with your brothers, Caro. No more secrets."

"But—"

"It is the right thing to do," he countered, removing his hand with the greatest of reluctance so he could button his shirt.

She nodded and stepped back. "As you wish."

* * *

There was something familiar about Jasper Sutton. He was tall also, dark-haired, and possessed a lethal air that could not be feigned.

He also looked as if he had recently been dragged from bed.

His hair was ruffled, his attire rumpled, eyes red-rimmed and bloodshot. He had the look of a man who had spent the evening before in dissolution. Fucking and drinking, unless Gavin was wrong. He did not think he was. There were some things he simply knew.

If only his name and his past were one of them.

"You wanted to speak with me," Caro's brother said. "Blue ruin?"

Sutton stalked to a sideboard in his office and poured two glasses of gin without waiting for an answer.

He cast a curious glance at Caro, who stood at his side. She sent him a small, apologetic smile. Her brother was a strange chap indeed. She was toying with her skirts, twisting the muslin in her agile fingers, a habit he had noted on more than one occasion. When a man could not recall his past, he had no choice but to notice everything.

"I don't know if I like blue ruin," he said, thinking he wanted a lucid mind for the discussion ahead.

"Everyone likes gin," Sutton countered, pressing a filled glass into his hand. "Drink it up. 'Tis excellent stores, and I don't waste it on everyone."

Tentatively, he sniffed the glass. He wondered if the man he had been before cared for spirits. But then, he realized it didn't matter. All that mattered in this moment was the man he was now, such as he was.

He took a sip. The stuff was wretched. He spat it back

into the glass, sputtering as the small amount he had managed to swallow burned down his throat.

"Christ." Disgust colored Sutton's voice as he frowned. "Everyone always loves a flash of lightning."

He coughed, catching his breath as Caro moved nearer and patted him gently on the back, as if to ease his suffering.

"Seems I don't," he croaked.

"Ain't surprising." Sutton's lip curled as he reclaimed the glass. "I'd drink it myself, but your spittle is swimming in it."

His bloody throat was still burning. "Apologies."

That was a decisive answer. The man he was now did *not* like gin. No more of that swill, thank you.

Sutton returned the glass to the sideboard before turning back to them, taking a sip of his own drink and swallowing it with a calm that bespoke a man who was more than familiar with the drink. "Now, then. You've a lot to answer for. Best get around to it as I don't 'ave all day. My sister tells me she's been keeping you in her chamber."

He noted that, like Caro, Jasper Sutton seemed to have an interesting pattern of speech. Part smooth, part rough, East End. The accent was familiar. So, too, the streets. He felt certain he was no stranger to the rookeries.

"She has not been staying with me," he hastened to reassure Jasper Sutton. "She selflessly surrendered her bed when she found me bleeding and ready to cock up my toes in the street. I owe her my life."

"So she's told me as well." Sutton scowled. "Caro is our healer. Soft heart, that one. Any man who dares crush it will be crushed by me."

Damnation. Thoughts of the kisses they had shared earlier rose in his mind, and he had no doubt Jasper Sutton could read the guilt etched on his face. Even now, as they faced her brother together, Caro at his side, the desire he felt for her was burning steady and bright within him. It could neither be tamed nor doused.

It was the only thing he did feel which he knew was true.

The rest, these fragments of memory which could have been dreams or pieces of his past...he knew not what they meant. Truth and falsehood had blended. The past ceased to exist. All he had was here. Now.

Her.

"I'll not crush it," he said roughly, meaning every word.

Caro was an angel. His angel. She had saved him. Nothing she could do would lessen his opinion of her.

Sutton eyed him, as if he did not dare trust him. "See that you don't, sir. Now, our Caro has saved you and kept you a secret as she nursed you back to health. But she tells me you aren't happy being treated like a king. Is that true?"

There was undeniable menace lacing the man's words.

"Jasper," Caro chastised. "I never said that, and you know it."

Sutton drained the rest of his glass and stared at them both, unrepentant. "Might as well've done."

"I want to earn my keep for staying here, and I would like to leave Caro's chamber so it is restored to her. Do you have a room I might rent?" he asked.

"Earn your keep?" Sutton laughed grimly. "*Caro*, is it? Sister, I'll thank you to keep your distance from 'im like a lady."

Caro stiffened and took a hasty step away. He mourned the loss of her touch and nearness both.

"Jasper, he wants to work for The Sinner's Palace. He'll do anything."

"He'll do nothing," her brother countered, unsmiling, before pinning a glare back upon him. "See 'ere, sir. Someone wanted you dead. More than one someone, if the injuries you had are an indication. I've been keeping you in my hell. What do you suppose that means for me, when your enemies find out Jasper Sutton's been hiding you?"

The man's question sank its claws into him.

What did it mean, indeed? All this time, he had been so consumed by trying to remember the man he had been, by regaining his strength and healing, and by thoughts of Caro, that he had spent precious little of his efforts on fretting over the reason he had been attacked. He had told himself it was likely a footpad. But Jasper Sutton's words had him wondering anew. If someone had been truly trying to kill him, and if that someone discovered he had not died in the attack, it stood to reason that the unknown foe would return. And that danger would follow.

"I would never put Caro or any of you at risk." He winced as he realized he had once more referred to her in familiar terms before her disapproving brother.

"If you don't want to bring peril here to The Sinner's Palace, where we've done nothing but protect you and stitch your hide back together, then you'll stay where you are," Sutton said.

"Trapped in a room like a prisoner?" he demanded, feeling the sudden need to flex his fingers. To form fists.

A strange urge, that.

It reminded him of the brief flash he'd had, of punching someone. Of relishing the crunch of bone.

"Here now. No one said you need to be trapped in a room." Sutton sauntered back to the sideboard and replenished his gin before turning toward them once more. "You can travel in the private halls of The Sinner's Palace rather than the public, but Randall needs to follow you and make certain you're doing what you're told. I'll not be having you bring trouble down upon us."

Relief washed over him. This man was harsh, but he seemed fair.

"I have no wish to bring any trouble upon any of you. All I want is to earn my keep and to be allowed to roam beyond the four walls which are driving me to the brink of madness."

It was true. Slipping from the room today had shown him just how much he required freedom of movement. He was grateful for Caro's hospitality. She had given him her chamber, her bed, and she had saved his life. Which was more than he deserved. Far more.

But he wanted more, it was true. He wanted to be able to escape those walls that had protected him for the duration of his stay. As a man who was no longer an invalid, he could not bear to remain trapped.

"I'll find a means for you to earn your bread here," Sutton said slyly. "All you need to do is keep your arse where it belongs. Until we can discover who you are or who was trying to send you to Rothisbone, you need to play this game my way."

He could accept that.

He nodded, stealing a glance at Caro, who was watching him with a mournful expression he could not define. "Aye. We'll play it your way, Mr. Sutton."

Caro's brother grinned and tossed back the rest of his gin. "Plummy. It's a square thing. But be warned that if you touch any of my sisters, I'm going to lop off your ballocks."

Well, hell.

CHAPTER 6

On a sigh, Caro carefully traveled back to Logan's chamber, which she was still using as her own. The hour was late. Her feet ached. And the wig atop her head—why, it felt as if it held the weight of the damned world.

Mayhap it did.

Days had passed since Caro had last seen Gavin. Jasper—curse him—had seen to that. Her brother was as protective as he was observant, and he had not approved of the familiarity between herself and Gavin the day they had confronted Jasper together in his office. Instead of working in her tiny room on creating new healing remedies before they were needed, she had been tasked with the entertainment of their patrons.

Ordinarily, Pen donned the requisite costumes and wigs to sing for the fancy lords who dedicated themselves and their purses to pursuing pleasure at The Sinner's Palace. But since Pen had suddenly become ill and confined to her bed—suspicious timing indeed if you asked Caro—the evening concerts had become Caro's burden.

Pen claimed she had a cough.

Caro believed their brother had somehow involved their sister in his secretive schemes.

When Caro had objected to Jasper's request that she take on her sister's role, her brother had calmly told her she had no choice in the matter unless she wanted herself, her siblings, and everyone in their employ to starve.

It had been hyperbole, and she knew it. The Suttons had fought long and hard to earn their place as the owners of one of the most sought-after gaming hells in London. *The Sinner's Palace offers unique entertainment unlike any other hell, and it is part of what has made us so bloody lucrative*, Jasper had said. *If there is no Madame Teulet singing like a goddamn sparrow, then there are no lords distracted from the green baize and losing all their papas' blunt.*

But like any sparrow, Caro did not like having to sing upon command. Nor did she appreciate all the time she was being forced to spend away from Gavin, who was now being allowed to wander, albeit in the private areas only.

Still, she worried over him. If the wrong person recognized him, all the care she had taken in nursing him back to health would have been for naught. And if something were to befall him...

Her heart would be dashed to bits like a small boat on the rocky shoals of a beach in a maelstrom. The plain truth of the matter was that she cared for Gavin Winter. Regardless of how much she had tried to remain aloof. Despite all the reasons why she should not. And no matter that she was deceiving him, the weight of her guilt becoming increasingly oppressive as the days dragged on and her lies grew.

At long last, she ventured into her chamber, the door clicking behind her.

And that was when she noticed she was not alone.

She would have screamed had not the interloper been so familiar. And handsome.

As it was, she nearly said his name aloud.

Instead, she pressed a hand over her heart as she took in the sight of him lying on her bed. Asleep, bless his heart. He must have come here in search of her and decided to await her return. Along the way, the wait had become too long. The low flickering of the brace of candles illuminated his features. She had watched him sleep on many occasions before, but now that his health had largely been restored, there was a marked difference.

Caro crossed the chamber, stopping at the bedside to gaze down at him. His dark hair hung over his brow—it had already been long, but it was getting longer now. His jaw was sharp and wide, angled like his cheekbones, his lips full and sensual. And now she knew how that mouth felt moving over hers.

Transcendent.

But she must not think of that now. Nor must she allow him to linger here. Jasper had required his guards to be extra vigilant after her joint trip with Gavin to his office. In his curt, gruff manner, Jasper had merely warned her with two words.

No bastards.

Now that she thought upon it, she could not be certain if her brother had been advising her to stay away from Gavin because he was a bastard Winter or if he was cautioning her against engaging in activity that would lead to her having a child out of wedlock. Both, she supposed.

Gently, she shook Gavin's shoulder to wake him. How she wished she could call him by name, and that she could confess everything to him. But Jasper had insisted they maintain this ruse for a bit longer, and she was bound by her promise to him.

Gavin jolted awake, blinking sleepily up at her. "Caro?"

He frowned as he took in her blonde wig and revealing dress. "What the devil are you wearing?"

She was aware of how she looked in the dress—her bosom pushed high and full out the top, all the better for their patrons to ogle her as she serenaded them. She withdrew her hand and tugged at her bodice, but it was a futile war she waged. The dress was tight, her stays designed to force her breasts heavenward. There was to be no modesty dressed as she was.

"I am wearing a gown, of course," she said, frowning back at him. "What are you doing in my bed?"

"Sleeping." He rose into a sitting position, and she could not help but to notice how much of the bed he occupied with his massive frame.

For some reason, although he had been staying in her bed for the duration of his time at The Sinner's Palace, she had not placed any emphasis upon it. He had been desperately wounded when he had arrived, and she had been so consumed with seeing to his care that she had scarcely been aware he was a man. But there was something deliciously intimate about the sight of him, his cheeks flush with color, his body replenished, in her bed.

He was watching her, scowling absently as his green gaze roamed over all the bare skin she had on display. She wished he had not seen her dressed as she was. What must he think of her?

Banishing the thought, she twisted her fingers in the skirts of her scarlet gown. "Of course you were sleeping. That was plain as the nose on my face. But it does nothing to explain why you were sleeping *in my bed*."

He grinned, and it was so boyish, so handsome, she felt the effect of it to her toes. "There is nothing about your nose —or any part of you for that matter—which is plain. And I sleep in your bed each night, unless you have forgotten."

Despite the accuracy of his statement and the innocence of it, her face flamed. "You are being unlike yourself this evening."

"Am I?" He scrubbed a hand over his jaw. "Deuced impossible to know what is like myself and what isn't, wouldn't you say? But I could say the same for you. I waited hours for you, and you never arrived, only to turn up dressed as a ladybird."

A ladybird. Was that what she looked like? She glanced down at herself and had to admit it was. She had felt like one this evening as well. So many eyes had been upon her. So many lascivious comments had been called as she sang.

"I needed to entertain our patrons this evening," she said, chancing a glance back at Gavin and hoping she would not read disgust or disapproval in his expression.

"I thought you were the healer." Gavin's eyes narrowed. "What manner of entertaining were you expected to perform? Does your brother truly demand this of you? I'm bloody outraged, Caro. I ought to beat him to a pulp on your behalf."

Gavin was broader of form than Jasper, but she had no doubt that if the two men were to battle against each other, they would be fairly evenly matched in terms of size and strength. Gavin's reputation as a champion prizefighter, however, did not bode well for her brother.

She tugged at her bodice once more, feeling increasingly irritated with her costume by the moment. "You were never to have seen me thus."

Her grumbled words of irritation had him rising from the bed altogether to tower over her. "I was never to have seen you at all, any longer, was I?"

There it was—the acknowledgment of the time that had passed between them.

She wanted to touch him. To throw herself into Gavin's arms. But her bloody wig was itching her head.

Caro sighed. "My brother is being protective."

His lip curled. "Doesn't look that way to me."

He was not wrong to make assumptions based upon her appearance. "My head is hot and I need to remove these curls before I swoon."

"Christ, woman, let me help you." He was scowling once more as he took her hand in his and led her to a chair, putting gentle pressure on her shoulders until she dutifully sat.

There was a small looking glass facing her, reflecting both of them. She was at once reminded of how much flesh she was showing and of how handsome he was, despite the fact he was frowning with displeasure.

"How many ladies have you helped to remove their wigs?" she asked, intending to lighten the mood between them but instantly realizing her error in judgment.

The words had been spoken. Too late to recall them.

He met her gaze in the looking glass. "I don't remember. I don't recall anything, in fact. My memory remains a jumble of emptiness and questions."

She bit the inside of her cheek, thinking that he had made some progress, minor recollections. Not enough, however. She would have expected more by now. There was the possibility he would never recall his past.

Caro yearned to tell him everything. His name, his past, who he was. She owed him the truth, and he deserved it.

"I am sorry," she said instead.

His hands were on her wig now, surprisingly tender for a man who was so large. But then, that was Gavin Winter, wasn't it? An endless source of amazement. And tenderness, too.

She could lose her heart to him so easily.

Heavens, what if she already had?

His fingers were unerringly finding all her hair pins, pulling them free. "Why should you be sorry? 'Tis whoever attempted to kill me who ought to be sorry. Mayhap I'll meet the cove someday, give him what he deserves."

A shiver passed through her at the notion of him facing whoever had committed such violence upon him. "You should not seek out such a madman, or madmen. You suffered so many wounds that I doubt one man could have inflicted them all. Especially considering you…"

She had been about to say considering his proficiency at sparring. One of the most victorious prizefighters in England would not be defeated with ease. But she could not say any of that. Because doing so would mean revealing she knew who he was. And she had to keep the truth from him. At least for a bit longer.

"Considering?" Gavin prodded as he removed another handful of pins which had been holding the wig in place.

"Considering your size and strength," she improvised, hating herself for the continuation of the lies.

"Mayhap I was soused," he suggested, pulling another errant pin until the wig was loose, sliding about atop her head. "Or I was attacked from behind."

"I considered those possibilities as well," she admitted quietly, watching in the looking glass as he lifted the wig from her head.

"But you decided against them?" He carried the wig as if it were a creature, depositing it atop the chest which housed her looking glass.

"Not entirely." Caro shifted in her seat, feeling distinctly uncomfortable thanks to their topic of discussion. "In the end, I could not be certain what happened. All I knew was that I ventured upon a man I presumed to be dead until I took a closer look and realized your chest was rising and falling. I am heartily glad you were not dead, and that I discovered you in time."

He turned back to her. "As am I, sweet Caro, which reminds me. I may not be able to recall a thing from my past, but I *can* remember that I have a gift for you."

A gift? For her? No one had ever given her something. Nor did she deserve one from this man. This wonderful, handsome, caring, sweet man to whom she lied each day.

She swallowed. "You need not give me a gift."

"It is the least I can do after the kindness and concern and healing you have bestowed upon my miserable arse." He grinned, and it was lopsided.

And her heart seemed to flip upside down.

Oh, Gavin.

"I am the healer here; tending to the injured is my job," she felt compelled to say, for it was the truth.

She would have aided anyone she had found wounded and beaten and bloodied. But she would not have lied to them. Should not have lied to *him*.

He reached into his waistcoat pocket and extracted a small object, holding it out for her. "I made this. For you."

Biting her lip against another rush of guilt, she accepted the offering, turning it over in her palm. It was smooth, hewn of wood. And it was exceptional. Easily the most intricate piece she had ever beheld.

"A butterfly? You carved this?"

His smile faded. "Aye, as a small means of expressing my thanks for all you've done for me. I meant to give it to you before now, but I haven't seen you for days."

"Did you miss me?" she teased.

"Aye," he said solemnly. "I did."

She had missed him too.

Her heart gave a pang. She wished she could tell him. Wished she did not have to perpetuate this lie. Wished she were not hopelessly caught between her duty to her family and the feelings she had developed for the man before her.

She rubbed her thumb over the details in the wings. "Thank you. It is beautiful."

"As are you."

Their gazes held, his simmering with promise. She could not look away. There was so much she wanted to say. So much she could not.

"I shall treasure this always," she said softly instead. "You are talented."

He shrugged his broad shoulders, wincing when his injury must have given him some pain. "Apparently I am. I had little else to do, and Randall gave me a blade and some wood. My hands seemed to have a mind of their own."

He had remembered how to carve and create. Surely that was a good sign.

"Did you have any other memories?" she asked, hopeful.

"I have one memory which has been haunting me."

"That sounds promising indeed." She traced the patterns on the butterfly, unable to look away from Gavin. "What have you remembered?"

"It is a new memory." He plucked the butterfly from her grasp and settled it on the chest holding her looking glass before turning back to her. He took her hands in his, twining their fingers together before gently tugging her to her feet. "My lips on yours. Do you recall?"

Oh.

"Yes." The admission fled her in a husky whisper. He had placed her hands on his chest, and she absorbed his warmth and strength, his vitality. "I have thought of little else."

* * *

CARO'S WORDS twined around his heart and held tight, clinging like an ivy vine. They were what he needed to hear. And Caro herself? Good Lord, she was all he wanted.

Kissing her again had not been his intention in seeking her out. But now that he had her in his arms, he could not deny the intensity of the longing coursing through him. It felt like a lifetime had passed since he had last seen her.

"May I kiss you again soon?" he asked, though playing the gentleman was killing him.

A small smile curved the lush fullness of her lips. "You did not ask permission the last time."

So he had not.

That sobered him. "I ought to have done, Caro. The truth is, I do not know what manner of man I am. I could be anyone. You deserve far better than that."

"Hush." She lifted a finger to his lips, laying it against them. "You are *you*, and that is all I need to know."

Humility washed over him. *Hell*, the way she said it...she made him feel as if he were someone. He kissed the fleshy pad of the digit pressed to his mouth. "Caro."

Her name emerged as little more than a growl. His restraint was fading. What a surprise the evening had been thus far. He had intended to await her return from whatever business she had been attending. But when the wait had dragged on, his eyes had grown heavier. Lulled into the inviting haven of her bed, he had settled atop a counterpane which smelled faintly of her scent.

Her finger moved, traveling around his lips, tracing in much the same manner she had touched the butterfly he'd spent her absence carving. Had a woman ever moved him the way this one did? He would like to believe he would recall it if she had, that there would be some sort of instinctive, marrow-deep knowledge.

"You have a lovely mouth," she said.

Christ.

His cock went rigid in his trousers. "Not as lovely as yours."

He wanted her more than he wanted his next breath. But he knew he could not have her. Not completely. Not until he knew who he was.

What if I never know who I am? What if I never remember?

Indeed. What would he do then?

Curse the curious blank state of his mind. This was an interminable hell in which he lived, unable to recall the smallest of details with certainty, unknowing what manner of man he was, whether or not he was truly free to pursue her. What if he was married or had a betrothed? What if he was a criminal? Surely no good man would have been beaten and shot and left for dead in the streets.

He hated it. Because all he wanted was to revel in Caro. To make her his. To lose himself in the only part of his life that held any meaning, any significance.

Her.

For now, there remained more hair pins in her lustrous auburn locks, keeping them confined. He plucked at them with abandon, setting her gorgeous hair free until it flowed down her back with wild abandon, until it spilled in long curls over her shoulders and breasts.

"It is a sin, hiding your hair," he grumbled.

He was still agitated at waking to the sight of her dressed so rudely, the full creaminess of her bosom nearly falling out of her bodice, the transparent skirts, the golden-tressed wig. How dare Jasper Sutton expect his sister to dress like a strumpet and flit about the gaming hell thus?

Outraged was a proper word for it. Now that more time had passed since he had first awoken to find himself robbed of his memory, his mind was becoming sharper. Even if he still had no recollection of who he was, concentrating upon the people around him and the words being spoken was far easier than it had once been. Most of the fog inhabiting his mind had lifted, and he no longer found himself aimlessly searching for a word he wanted to use before speaking.

"Hiding my hair is part of the costume," she said softly, trailing her touch over his jaw now. "The gentlemen here prefer golden hair, Jasper says, and I must wear the wig."

"The gentlemen here are fools, and they do not deserve you." The worry that had been needling him since he had first opened his eyes to a vastly different Caro renewed. "You never did say what manner of entertainment he expects you to provide the patrons with."

If it was what he feared—that she was forced to flirt with them, or mayhap more—not even an angel descended from heaven was going to be sufficient to keep him from hunting down Jasper Sutton and slamming his fist into his face.

"I sing."

Relief hit him. "You sing. That is all?"

Her fingers were threading through the hair at his temple, and the touch was shy, tentative. But glorious just the same. "That is all. What did you suppose?"

"I don't want to say."

He did, however, want her to continue her gentle explorations. Her touch felt so damn good. Everything about her did. Good and right. Perfect, in fact.

"Ordinarily Pen sings. The wig and the dress are hers, but my sister has been plagued by a cough for the past few days." A frown furrowed her brow. "I will own, the timing is strange. I expect my brother Jasper has a hand in this."

"He does not want me to become too familiar with you," he said, because it had been painfully true that day in Sutton's office.

"He is protective." Her fingers continued their travel.

Heat slid down his spine as he finished removing the last

of the pins from her hair and sleek, fragrant tresses framed her face. "So protective, he forces his sisters to dress as doxies and sing for the lords who gamble away their fortunes and drink themselves to oblivion each night."

"Force is a strong word. The Sinner's Palace belongs to us all. Pen enjoys singing, while I enjoy healing. However, our voices are similar, and I know the songs."

Her fingers had reached his nape, and she was toying with the hair falling over his neck. He could not resist pressing a kiss to the smooth flesh of her inner arm. His hands found their way to her waist, hidden in the thin layers of her gown and petticoats. Her stays kept him from the inviting lushness of her curves.

"I don't like the notion of all those lords leering at you," he said.

Because it was true. And because, *damn it*, he hated to know this was what had been keeping her from him. Worse, that he was likely the cause.

"It is not as terrible as you suppose." Her fingers grazed over his skin.

There was a fever overtaking him, a fire in his blood that was entirely this woman's making. "You should be in your work room, doing what pleases you. Not singing for the pleasure of men who do not deserve to hear your voice."

The smile curving her lips was sad. "Sometimes we do things not because we want to, but because we must. Life is not always rife with the choices we wish."

Hell. How right she was. Although he had no memories of the man he had been before she had found him several weeks ago, the man he was now well understood the wisdom of her words. If he had his choice, he would regain his memory, know he was free to pursue Caro, and make her his wife.

Love.

That was the strangeness in his chest. The heaviness in his gut. The reason why Caro was all he could think about.

He had fallen in love with the woman who had brought him back from the dead. But he still didn't know if he was free to pursue her, if there was another he loved as the man he had been before. The man he could not recall.

His hold on her waist tightened with possession. She belonged here with him, damn it. He could not be wrong about that. "What have you done because you must, Caro?"

He wanted to know, and yet he did not, for fear of what she would reveal and the effect it would have upon his heart.

The fingers brushing over his neck stilled, and he felt her tensing in his arms. "I have been deceitful."

He found it difficult to reconcile his angelic butterfly with dishonesty. Impossible, in fact. "I know you, Caro. There must have been good reason."

Her smile was sad. "Your opinion of me is far too good. I do not deserve it."

"Yes." He gave her waist a gentle squeeze to emphasize his words. "You do. You are an angel, and you saved my life, butterfly. I shall never forget that, nor you. Not even, I like to think, should I take another blow to the head. If I were to lose every memory I owned again, I believe you would still be there."

She sifted his hair with a tenderness that planted itself in his heart like a seed. "Let us hope you shall never again suffer such a blow."

"Aye, let us hope that." He pressed a chaste kiss to her forehead, wanting to do so much more and yet not daring.

The hour grew late, and he knew it. He was ever aware of the problems he could cause for her, lingering in her chamber. If any of her family or The Sinner's Palace guards were to discover she was not alone, there would be hell to pay, and he did not want to cause any further troubles for her beyond what he had already done.

But when he would have moved away, she wound her arms around his neck, holding him there. Her hazel eyes were pinned upon him, and he thought again of how undeniable it was, this foreign emotion rising within him, lifting like an ascension balloon taking to the sky.

He had fallen in love with this woman.

He wanted to make her his wife.

"Is that the kiss you were after?" she asked softly.

Hesitantly.

His cock swelled at the huskiness in her voice, at her nearness, the way her scent danced over his senses. "For this evening, it is all the kiss I dare. I'll not make any more problems for you, Caro. You've done enough for me by nursing me back to health."

"You have a good heart." She paused, as if she was about to say more, and then shook her head. "Too good."

He released his hold on her waist and reached for her wrists, still around his neck, gently pulling her away though the movement caused pain to radiate from his wound. The bullet had done its damage, and while he was largely healed, he was not certain if he would ever move the injured arm without pain again.

Despite the agony tearing through him, he raised both her hands to his lips for another kiss, wishing he could offer more. So much more.

"My heart belongs to you." Before he said anything more foolish, he kissed her cheek. "Sleep well, sweet Caro."

And then he reluctantly released her and quit the room. Walking away required all the restraint he had.

CHAPTER 7

My heart belongs to you.

Had she truly heard those words last night? They seemed a dream by the harsh light of the morning as Caro walked to the carriage awaiting her in the mews. Pen was yet ill, and Caro had used nearly all her stores after nursing a string of wounded patients. There had been her brothers and their endless scrapes, a fit of coughing which had overtaken some of the kitchen workers and guards, and then there had been *him*.

Gavin Winter.

Her heart pounded at the thought of his name. At the remembrance of the manner in which he had gazed upon her last night, as if she were beloved to him. As if she were truly worthy of his adulation.

But she was not. And *bloody blue blazes*, she needed to collect herself. To remember to guard her heart and keep her distance from him as best she could from this moment on. He would return to the welcoming arms of the Winters, and he would hate her for who she was and for what she had done. The deceit she had perpetuated filled her with guilt.

Jasper could not forever keep Gavin Winter a secret, hidden away in the private quarters of The Sinner's Palace. Soon enough, the truth would need to be revealed, Gavin would know she had betrayed him, and he would never forgive her. Oh, how her heart ached this morning. She wanted to be filled with joy at Gavin's confession, but all she felt was worry.

Caro was so distracted she did not realize she was not the sole occupant of the carriage until she had seated herself on the bench, the door soundly closed at her back, and she found a pair of emerald eyes upon her.

"Ga—merciful angels and saints!" The exclamation left her, and her belly sizzled with pent-up anguish as she realized she had almost spoken his name aloud.

It had not been the first occasion for such a slip, either.

"I am neither an angel nor a saint, I trust." He winked, then grinned. "Common fame has it that I am a man, formed of flesh and blood. All too mortal. I nearly went to Rothisbone until an angel saved me."

The stone of guilt inhabiting her stomach seemed to double in size. "I am not an angel either, and I can assure you of that. But that is neither here nor there. What are you doing in my carriage?"

He gestured with his good hand, drawing her attention to his long legs and well-muscled thighs, so clearly outlined by the snugness of his trousers. "Sitting here, of course."

She sighed. He was so bloody charming, she could forget about all the reasons why he should not be in this carriage with her. The potential danger to him was chief among them.

"How did you know I was taking the carriage today?" she asked softly as the conveyance lurched into motion.

She had already informed Jerome, The Sinner's Palace coachman, where she was going. To the same apothecary she visited every few months. He was simply doing his duty. She wondered then if Gavin had been conspiring with the men in the Sutton family employ.

"Jerome told me." His grin deepened.

Gavin Winter was befriending everyone in The Sinner's Palace. She was not surprised. He was kind, caring, and sweet. He was a man who had overcome tremendous wounds, the likes of which would have proved the end of most. And yet, here he sat opposite her, trusting, handsome, beloved.

Everything within her froze at the word, the sentiment. Could it be that she had fallen in love with him?

"Caro?" Gavin's smile faded, turning into a concerned frown. "Are you displeased I am here? If you are worried your brother will discover I accompanied you this morning, you needn't fear. Jerome is a friend. He'll not carry any tales. I came directly to the carriage from the private quarters, and no one saw me."

That was not what had been worrying her most, but she leapt upon the excuse, which was far easier than admitting she had fallen in love with the handsome man seated opposite her.

But she had. The truth was there, in her heart, undeniable despite all the reasons why she should not love Gavin Winter. For as long as she could recall, the Winters had been the enemies of the Suttons. Recent relaxations in the tensions between their families had been promising, but all it would require was the Winters to discover Jasper had been secreting their missing brother from them for war to come raging in the East End.

Then, there was the matter of her continued deceit. With each day that passed as she knew Gavin's identity and kept it from him at her brother's request, another part of her shriveled away. The goodness in her that Philip had not destroyed was being decimated by the continued lie.

And Gavin was staring at her now, his expression open and unguarded. Trusting, even. She was not worthy of his confidence. Not worthy of his love.

"I trust Jerome," she managed.

The one she did not trust was herself. Because the more time she spent in Gavin's presence, the more her feelings for him deepened. The bond between them grew stronger by the day. And when they would be torn asunder, as inevitably they must...

Her heart would be devastated.

Gavin grinned, looking boyishly handsome, with a mischievous air she could not help but to find infectious. "Do you trust *me*?"

Too much.

This was a dangerous path they were traveling together.

"Yes," she admitted. "However, you must promise to remain in the carriage while I visit the apothecary."

He raised a dark brow, studying her. "How much longer will I be a prisoner, do you suppose?"

"You are not a prisoner," she denied with haste.

Too much haste.

Because it was true—truer than Gavin knew.

And she hated it.

He winced. "Feels that way. I'm a prisoner of my mind and a prisoner within four walls."

Her heart ached for him at his inability to recall who he was. "Have you had any more memories?"

He shook his head. "Nothing certain."

Hope stirred within her. "Something uncertain, then?"

"Murky bits."

"Such as?"

Mayhap she should not nudge him, but speaking of his memory was providing excellent distraction from the manner in which his big, muscled body seemed to inhabit nearly all the space of the carriage's interior.

"Violence," he said, succinct, his jaw tightening. "Nothing I care to remember, and it may be the beating I recall rather than anything from my past. Dreams plague me, and they are always the same."

Oh, Gavin.

How she loathed his suffering. How she wished she could somehow end it.

You can end it, whispered the voice within. Her conscience, she supposed. She should tell him the truth. She desperately needed to convince Jasper that revealing Gavin's identity to him was necessary.

"We needn't speak of it."

"I ain't afraid to talk." He sent her a careful smile. "But how long is the drive to your apothecary?"

"Half an hour." She visited a very particular shop, which was not in the East End at all.

But Caro had learned long ago that quality mattered when it came to healing. She would venture from the familiar confines of her part of London if it meant obtaining better materials.

"Come." He held out his hand to her, his broad palm facing up.

She stared at his hand and recalled what it felt like on her skin. This was madness. If she touched him, she would never be able to stop. "I am perfectly comfortable on this side of the carriage."

He cocked his head at her. "Are you afraid of joining me?"

He was devastatingly handsome. Singularly tempting. He was nothing like Philip, and everything a man should be. If only he could be hers.

"I am not afraid, but I do question your judgment. There is scarcely any room for me."

That was not a lie. Gavin Winter was massive. It was likely one of the traits which made him such a successful prizefighter.

"There is room aplenty here." A grin returned to his well-molded lips as he patted his lap with his other hand.

Heat slid through her. He wanted her to sit on him.

And she very much desired to do so.

"I am too heavy."

"You'll be light as the butterfly you are. Come, Caro."

She placed her hand in his, amazed at how much smaller hers was. He tugged, and she went willingly, settling herself on his lap.

* * *

CARO WAS WARM, soft, and sweet-scented, the supple curves of her rump teasing his senses. He never wanted to let her go. Taking care to position her so that she would not come into contact with the rude protrusion of his rigid cock, he settled her more comfortably against his chest. She turned toward him and the brim of her bonnet poked him in the eye.

"Oh dear!" she exclaimed, sounding adorably befuddled. "I did not mean for that to happen."

He gave her a wry grin, rubbing at his watering eye. "I'll live to see another day. At least, I think I will."

He was teasing her, but she frowned.

And as their gazes clashed and held, a flash of memory seemed to crash through his skull. The memory of a fist crashing into his eye, of it swelling shut. He knew what the blow felt like. Recalled not being able to see from the eye until the swelling had subsided.

She must have felt him tense beneath her, or read the expression on his face, because her hand was on his jaw, stroking as if to soothe. "What is the matter?"

He blinked, clearing the tears from his eye, and pressed a kiss to the center of her palm. "Nothing. I think I may have remembered something...someone hitting me in the eye."

"Who was it? Do you remember a face?" she asked, still gently stroking his jaw.

He searched the abyss of his mind for more details, but there were none to be reclaimed. "That is all I can recall, the force of the blow, my eye swelling shut. It was the same eye. Your bonnet reminded me."

"It is a handsome bonnet but I hardly expected it to have such power," she teased. "This is wonderful news, however. If some details return to you, surely others will follow."

"I hope so." He settled a hand on her waist and tapped on the brim of her bonnet with the other. The weight of her in his lap was delicious. "Do you think you might remove this until we reach the apothecary? I'd prefer to keep my eye."

She smiled, untied the ribbon beneath her chin, and then plucked the millinery from her head. "I would not wish to cause you harm. Not ever."

There was a sadness in her voice today, and he couldn't help but to suspect something was amiss. "No one discovered my visit to you, did they?"

By *no one*, he meant her brother Jasper in particular, who seemed to be the leader of the family. He had seen some of the other Sutton brothers in passing, and at least one sister—Pen. But Caro had told him there were seven siblings in all. There had been an eighth once, but she spoke of that brother with heartache, always referencing the past. He believed that brother was dead, but he hadn't wished to upset her by asking too many questions.

She shook her head, and this time, his eye was blessedly spared another altercation with her hat. "No. But we must not make a habit of such visits."

Pity, that. He wanted to spend every night in her chamber. All night long. To make her his wife and spend the rest of his life worshiping her as she deserved.

"I will try to stay away, but it isn't easy, Caro." His other hand settled on her waist at just the right moment, for the carriage hit a rut and swayed violently.

She clutched his shoulders, eyes going wide, clinging to him. "Bloody ballocks, that was a bump."

The moment the words left her lips, she went scarlet.

"So the angel has a sinner's tongue," he quipped, smiling as he drew her nearer.

Would it be too much to ask for another splendidly timed run over the old hasty pudding that resulted in her wrapping her arms around his neck?

"I've spent most of my life in a gaming hell," she said, still flushing. "I suppose it shows."

"I don't know where the devil I spent most of my life, but I do know where I want to spend what remains of it."

"Where?" she breathed.

"With you, Caro." He was sure he should not be making a declaration now, that it was too soon, that he didn't know enough about the man he had been before he had awoken in The Sinner's Palace. That everything could change if his memory returned. But the way he felt for her…it was strong and deep and true. "I've fallen in love with you, and I want to make you my wife."

The moment he said the words, he realized how foolish they sounded. He did not even have a name. Nor a ha'penny. What could a nameless man without a past offer to her?

"You've fallen in love with me," she repeated, her countenance dazed.

"Aye." He caressed her cheek. "I know I've nothing to my name. Hell, I don't even *know* my name. But I know my heart, Caro. I love you. I'll never feel for another what I feel for you."

Her eyes were glistening, the grays becoming more pronounced. "But you scarcely know me."

"I know enough of you to know you've the heart of an angel. You're kind and good, Caro Sutton."

"No," she said softly, sadly. "I'm not."

Of course she was, though if it was her humility prodding her response or her lack of desire to marry him, he could not be sure. He had thought she felt the same connection. She had certainly kissed him as if she had, and the budding tenderness between them could not be denied. However, it was possible he had spoken too soon. Or that she simply had no wish to wed a man with no memory.

Hell. How could he marry without a *name*? And there remained the troubling issue of whether or not he was free to wed her.

He stowed the troubling questions for now.

"If you do not feel the same, tell me." He searched her gaze, trying to make sense of the muddle he'd made with his loose tongue and overflowing emotions. Everything was new to him; he was a new person, and finding his footing was akin to walking on an icy lake.

"Of course I feel the same." She pressed her lips together, and a lone tear spilled down her cheek. "You must know I do. I love you, and it would be my honor to be your wife. But there is the matter of who you are, which must be addressed, and there is much you do not know about me, and…oh, what if your memories return and you find you do not like me at all?"

"That would never happen," he reassured her, for he knew it instinctively.

Nothing could alter the depths of emotion he felt for the woman in his arms.

"But what if it does?" she persisted, looking forlorn.

A second tear trailed down her cheek to join the first. He

kissed it away, catching the saltiness of her sorrow on his lips. "It won't, Caro. I vow it. I may not remember who I am, but I would never forget the way I feel for you. From the moment I woke and saw you, the bond between us has been undeniable, and it has only grown stronger. I know I have nothing to provide you now, but I am determined to make myself a worthy man for you. Only promise me you will give me the chance."

"I promise."

She cradled his face with a tender touch, and she kissed him. Hesitantly at first, and then with growing ardor. He groaned and took control, his lips moving against hers, the need to taste and claim her rising along with his cockstand. He teased the seam of her lips, then swept inside.

Sweet as honey.

So responsive.

Longing ripped through him as he deepened the kiss, and she shifted on his lap until he was nestled against the tempting swell of her rump. Her tongue teased his. For an unknown span of time, they kissed each other breathless. He forgot where they were, that any moment, they would arrive at their destination.

And then, the carriage rocked to a halt.

She broke the kiss, staring at him, her mouth swollen. "We are here."

"Aye." Reluctantly, he retrieved her bonnet and settled it atop her head. "We are."

He was greedy, and he wanted more of her, but he knew that he must be happy with what he had gotten and bide his time for more.

If only he could remember who the bloody hell he was.

CHAPTER 8

For the second time that day, Caro found herself being tugged into a masculine lap. However, this time, it was not a place where she wanted to be, because the man into whose lap she had landed was not Gavin Winter. Instead, it was Viscount Derby, a lord who had been ogling her with a lascivious stare for the entirety of her performance that evening. Whereas being held so close by Gavin had felt at once comforting, familiar, and exciting, Lord Derby's arms tightening around her waist only caused alarm to rise within her.

"My lord," she said, attempting to pry his hands from her, "you must let me go. My songs for the evening are finished."

"I'll make you sing a different ditty altogether," the lord growled in her ear, before pressing a wet kiss to her throat.

He smelled of spirits and tobacco and…cheese.

Detestable creature.

She tugged at his hands some more, but that only seemed to heighten his enjoyment. "Lord Derby, please release me."

"You want my cock," he proclaimed in a low voice.

"You've been begging for it all evening, and I'm going to give it to you, my pretty little whore."

Caro cast a frantic glance around the private room where she had been singing this evening, but neither Jasper nor any of her other brothers was anywhere to be found. Timothy was acting as guard, but a conflict between two patrons had distracted him. Randall was likely continuing to guard Gavin. Which meant she was alone. The other patrons in the room were drinking and playing at cards, and the lords at Derby's table were looking on with ill-disguised amusement.

"If your cock gets anywhere near me, I'll cut it off," she warned as his hand wandered to cup her breast through her stays.

"Looks as if Madame Teulet does not want to play slap and tickle with you, Derby," observed one of the others in a mild tone that suggested this was by no means the first time Lord Derby had accosted a female in their presence.

She wondered if the lord had ever done so to Pen. And if so, why had Pen never said a word about such egregious behavior? The viscount had not been in the private room for any of her performances thus far, so Caro had no comparison. In her experience, some men turned into leering, revolting monsters when they were soused. Mayhap Derby was one of those wretches.

"She'll change her mind soon enough," Derby announced to his friend. In her ear, he spoke again, the words directed at Caro alone. "How much coin to have you for the night, love?"

"You cannot have me." She struggled, managing to wrest an arm free of his cloying grasp, and then slapped the hand that was squeezing her breast. "You cannot have me tonight, and you cannot have me ever. I am not for sale, my lord. If you are seeking entertainment, one of the other ladies here will be happy to aid you."

The hell had ladybirds aplenty. Caro was simply not one of them.

"I've had them all," Derby said, shifting in his seat so that the tumescence in his trousers rubbed against her. "I want you now. I love that husky, sweet voice of yours. I want to hear it calling my name."

She was going to be ill. Caro managed to land an elbow in the viscount's ribs, and she knew a moment of satisfaction as the breath hissed from his lungs and he howled with pain. Sooner or later, someone would appear in the room and come to her aid. But she was not about to be mauled by this dunderhead in the meantime.

"Saucy bitch," he cursed with a low grunt. "I'll teach you to harm your betters."

With that warning, he caught a handful of her blonde wig and tugged viciously.

The pins holding it in place tore at her hair with unmerciful vengeance, bringing tears to her eyes. "Release me, you despicable cur."

"I'll release you when I'm ready, Madame." He tugged at her wig again, and this time pulled it free. He held it aloft. "What the devil?"

Caro felt strangely naked, as if she had been stripped bare before them.

The wig was part of her costume. When she wore it, she was not Caro but Madame Teulet. And now, this blighter had stripped even that dignity from her.

"Give me that, you scoundrel." She had forgotten long ago that she was never to insult their patrons. The viscount was a vile creature, and she would call upon Jasper to forbid him from returning.

Caro reached for the wig but froze when a deep, familiar voice laden with menace rose behind them.

"If I were you, I would do as the lady says. I would also let her go, as she plainly has no wish to be accosted by a booby in his altitudes like you."

She turned with a combination of relief and trepidation to find Gavin towering over them. He looked every bit as ferocious as the sting in his voice. When he was angry, he was almost frightening. She could see the warrior in him, fierce and determined.

A myriad of questions hit her startled mind. How had he found her? Did he not realize he wasn't meant to be wandering about the public halls and rooms of the hell? What if someone recognized him?

His appearance must have shocked Derby as well, for the viscount released his hold on Caro enough that she could free herself. She shot to her feet and rushed to his side. He glanced down at her, his features as hard as if they had been hewn from granite.

"Did he hurt you?" he demanded.

"No," she said, not wishing for further trouble.

Gavin looked as if he were about to commit murder.

"Who the hell are you?" Derby demanded, still seated, though red-faced now, a slight slur to his words that proved just how much drink he had consumed that evening.

"Damned if I know," Gavin said grimly. "But what I do know is that a cove can't go about accosting the ladies in this fine establishment. If you can't follow the rules, you're going to have to go."

"Is that so?" the viscount asked, looking amused.

"Aye." Gavin glared at him, flexing his fingers as if he longed to form a fist. "It is. Amuse yourself with ladies who are interested from this moment on. Though I bloody well doubt you'll find any."

With that parting shot, Gavin slid a comforting arm around Caro's waist and led her from the room. When they had reached the safety of the private halls, he turned to her, frowning, his gaze searching and concerned. "Are you certain that bastard didn't hurt you?"

She shivered, grateful that Gavin had arrived when he had, and thankful too that he had not punched the lord, though she had been certain his instinct had called for it. "I am certain. Thank you for coming to my rescue."

"Where is your cursed brother?" he demanded. "Where are any of them? Or the bloody guards for that matter? There should have been no need for a rescue, Caro."

"All the same, I am glad you were there." It was her turn to frown as she thought of the potential danger he had brought upon himself. Surely some of the gentlemen in The Sinner's Palace tonight had watched the famed Gavin Winter in a prizefight. "But you should not have gone into the public rooms. You may have placed yourself in jeopardy by doing so."

"And I would do it again in a moment if it meant keeping you out of the clutches of a bastard like that." He shook his head, his fists clenched at his sides. "When I saw him touching you and how you struggled to escape him and heard what he was saying to his cronies…hell, Caro. I wanted to acquaint him with my fists. I was filled with rage and violence. I remember how it felt to pummel someone. To square off with an opponent. I knew if I would have hit him, I wouldn't have stopped."

His reaction made sense. He had been a prizefighter. Some parts of him remained, hiding. It was only a matter of time until all his memories returned to him, she had no doubt.

Fear curled around her heart, joining the ever-present guilt. This morning in the haven of the carriage, when she had been wrapped in his strength and he had been gazing at her with so much raw, unfettered love, she had allowed herself to believe there could be a future for the two of them.

That she could become his wife as he had asked. But the truth remained, painful and dangerous, burning like a hot coal in the pit of her belly.

This situation was untenable. She was going to have to break her promise to Jasper. Gavin had already been seen in the public rooms of The Sinner's Palace, potentially inviting great peril to himself. If word spread, keeping his presence a secret would no longer be necessary. Moreover, they owed him the truth.

"Say something, Caro," Gavin implored, shaking her from the tumult of her thoughts.

"Thank you. I am glad you did not hit him. He is a lord, and it would not have gone well for you if you had done that."

"He is a fucking swine, is what 'e is."

The vehemence in Gavin's voice, the epithet, and the dropped *h* told her just how distraught he was. It also told her that more of him was returning. Her time with him was limited. So terribly, horribly limited.

What will happen if he remembers everything tonight? Tomorrow?

She tried to shake the questions from her mind, but they remained, probing, mocking.

I will lose him. I will lose him, but he will regain himself.

"You must not worry yourself over it," she said, reaching for his fists, taking them in her hands. "Nothing happened."

"But it bloody well could have. Where was everyone who's meant to be protecting you, damn it?" Fury still emanated from him, but he did not pull away from her touch, and gradually, his hands relaxed, his fingers lacing through hers.

"Why were you in the private room?" she asked, needing to distract him as much as she needed to distract herself. "You never said."

Color swept over his high cheekbones, and she realized it was the first time she had ever witnessed him flush. "I wanted to hear you sing, but I was too late. All I saw was that whoreson molesting you."

He was so sweet, her Gavin. Even if he could never truly be hers. Could she not pretend? At least for this evening, while they still had time and each other?

"I will sing for you if you like," she offered. "Come to my chamber again tonight."

His gaze darkened to vibrant, emerald green, and heat flared in her belly. "That's an invitation I can't resist."

And that was when she realized she wanted to give him more than a song. She wanted to give him herself, her body. He already owned her heart.

"Meet me there in an hour's time?" She tried to smile past the sudden rush of yearning tearing through her.

That ought to be sufficient time to remove her revealing gown and don something of her own. She also didn't dare any of her siblings or the guards catching sight of Gavin entering her chamber with her.

"There is nowhere I would rather be. But first, we are going to see your brother, Caro."

He had not surrendered his need to speak with Jasper, it would seem. That was just as well, because she needed to speak to Jasper about Lord Derby's conduct. She feared for Pen and for the ladies in their employ.

"We will go together," she agreed, though she knew Jasper would be outraged when he discovered Gavin had been in the public rooms.

Facing her brother alone just now felt too daunting, and Gavin wore the expression of a man who would not be swayed.

"Together." The smile Gavin bestowed upon her made her heart ache. "I like the sound of that."

So did she.

Far, far too much.

But she did not say that, because she was going to revel in every moment she could still pretend Gavin Winter was hers.

* * *

He was beginning to dislike Jasper Sutton.

He was also beginning to dislike the guards at The Sinner's Palace, one of whom was currently planted before the door to Sutton's office and pinning him with a stern glare.

"We need to speak with Miss Sutton's brother," he repeated. "Hell, not necessarily even this one. Any of them. Someone needs to know what happened tonight."

The guard looked distinctly unimpressed. "What 'appened?"

He scowled. "That is none of your affair. Bloody hell, man, will Sutton not make time for his own sister?"

"Aye. When 'e finishes with the lady visitor."

A growl tore from him, and the desire to ram his fist into someone's nose, which had been simmering beneath the surface of his tensions from the moment he had seen that despicable lord with Caro in his lap, rose to a crescendo. "Do you mean to tell me Sutton is in there bedding a ladybird when his own sister was being abused in the public rooms?"

Caro laid a staying hand on his arm, but the fires of his fury had ignited once more.

The guard shrugged, giving him an insolent grin. "Not my concern what Sutton does in 'is office or who with."

"We can return later," Caro offered.

"No," he countered, still eying the smirking guard. "We won't. We will wait."

The guard remained where he was, apparently finding the situation amusing. "As you like."

"My brother is..." Caro paused as she sought the proper words. "He can become distracted by feminine companionship."

He was not the only one suffering from such a malady. But he had a feeling his distraction was one hell of a lot more innocent than Jasper Sutton's.

"He deserves a cuff to the head," he told her, meaning every word and intending to deliver upon the threat, too. "On your behalf. He is meant to be protecting you, and he is not doing his duty."

"Someone would have found me," she said quietly, in the same tone of voice she had used when he had been an invalid, out of his mind with fever, and she had attempted to calm him.

Soothing, dulcet tones. They had lulled him into tranquility before, but he would not be swayed now. This was too damned important. *She* was too important.

"And what if no one had?" he demanded, outraged on her behalf. "What if I had not attempted to hear you sing? What if that bastard had hurt you, Caro? I'll not stand by and allow this to happen to you again."

A stern rap sounded from the inside of the door, followed by a series of knocks in an unusual pattern. The guard's shoulders straightened. "Sutton's finished 'is business now."

Business? Is that what he called bedding women whilst his innocent sister was almost being defiled by vain, arrogant lordlings? More outrage surged, doubling the overwhelming quantity already within him.

He was seething with fury. Mayhap instead of a cuff to the ear, he would slam his fist into Sutton's nose. There was no sound quite like that of a man's beak breaking. He had broken a nose before. He knew it. And suddenly, a hazy, indistinct memory returned to him. A ginger-haired man, facing him with fists raised. He threw a punch and the man's nose gushed with blood.

But as quickly and unexpectedly as the memory returned, it dissipated, leaving only nothingness in its wake.

"Is something amiss?" Caro hissed at his side.

His entire body was tense, and it was not entirely from outrage. With a jolt, he returned to the present, looking down at her upturned face. There was so much concern and tenderness in her countenance.

His butterfly.

"A memory returned to me just now," he told her. "At least, that is what I think it was."

Often, it was deuced difficult to determine dream from memory, or to know whether or not these tiny splinters that arrived in his mind were recollections of his life or they were the fancies of his addled mind. Fortunately, he felt quite sharp in his knowledge box these days.

Her brow furrowed, her hazel eyes searching his. "What manner of memory?"

Violence. Always violence. What the hell did that mean? And what did that make him? *Christ.* Who else but a criminal would nearly cock up his toes in an alley behind an East End gaming hell?

Before he could answer her, the door to Jasper Sutton's office opened, stealing his attention. The guard stepped aside, and a dark-haired woman dressed in an elegant gown swept over the threshold.

There was no mistaking the swelling of her mouth or the redness on her pale skin, which had undoubtedly been caused by Jasper Sutton's whiskers. His irritation soared once more. The hell of it was, the lady did not look at all as he had expected a ladybird would. Her gown was modest and well-fashioned of fine fabric, with spangles adorning it and silver embroidery. There were jewels at her throat, and kid gloves covered her hands.

Sutton sauntered over the threshold next, his gaze fixed upon the lady who was fleeing his lair. The bastard looked smug, in stark contrast to the lady's bashfulness.

"Lady Octavia," he said to her, and she stilled, glancing back.

What the hell was unfolding here? Jasper Sutton had been locked away in his office, kissing a *lady*?

The lady in question halted and pivoted to face Sutton. "Yes, Mr. Sutton?"

"I did not agree to aid you in this madcap plan of yours."

A small smile crept over the lady's countenance. "You will, sir."

Sutton's eyes narrowed. "I won't."

"If you will not help me, I will find another who shall," the woman countered calmly. "But now, the hour does grow late, and I fear my sister will go fretting over me. I must go."

"My lady," Sutton called when she would have gone, staying her once more.

"Mr. Sutton, I have already told you that I must go," she said, her voice firm and almost scolding.

"See that one of my guards follows you home," Sutton said, then turned to the guard who stood to the side of his office door. "Hugh, make certain to follow my guest. I'll not have any harm coming to her."

Lady Octavia rolled her eyes heavenward. "Sutton, I told you, I do not need your protection. I travel about London as I wish, and no harm has ever befallen me."

Sutton glared. "It won't start on my watch."

"As you wish." The lady shrugged. "I shall see you tomorrow."

"I'll not be here," Sutton growled.

She ignored him and moved down the corridor with the

commanding elegance of a queen, the guard—Hugh—following in her wake.

At last, Sutton turned his attention away from the woman he had been kissing and Lord knew what else in his office. "What do you want? Caro, where is your wig, and why the hell is so much of your bosom hanging out of your bloody gown?"

Fine time for the bastard to take note of his sister.

He stepped forward, intent upon setting the matter straight. "You are forcing your sisters to dress like ladybirds and sing for your patrons whilst you are playing at tossing up petticoats. Do you know that one of those bleeding lords was intent upon forcing himself on Caro this evening? She is goddamned lucky I came upon her when I did."

Sutton went ashen, his gaze flitting to his sister. "Caro? What the devil? Who did it? I'll have the bastard banished from the hell."

"It was Viscount Derby," Caro said. "Have you had complaints about him from others?"

Sutton's lip curled. "This will be the last complaint I receive about him. That's a promise. But as for you, patient, what the hell were you doing in the public rooms? I've warned you not to cause trouble."

"I would apologize but I'm not sorry I was there to help Caro. She won't be singing for the entertainment of your patrons any longer, either."

Sutton's eyes narrowed as he regarded him, stroking his jaw. "You're a bold one ain't you, patient?"

The name irked him. He wanted to know who he was, damn it.

"I'm a *protective* one," he corrected grimly. "Someone has to look after her. You and your siblings had thrown her to the wolves."

"Timothy was on duty tonight," Sutton said, addressing Caro once more. "Did you not see him?"

Caro shook her head. "One of the patrons accused another of cheating, and he'd gone to investigate. He hadn't returned."

"Curse it." Sutton rubbed his jaw some more. "I'll speak with him, and I'll add guards to the floor."

"Damned right you will," he said, still furious over what could have happened to Caro and what she'd had to endure.

Sutton's look turned speculative. "And what're you doing chasing after my sister, patient? Didn't I warn you to keep your distance?"

He raised a brow. "You can be glad I didn't listen."

A sharp laugh tore from the other man. "Christ. I'm starting to *like* you."

He supposed that was a compliment, but with a man like Jasper Sutton, one could never be sure. Then again, with a missing memory, one couldn't be sure of anything at all.

CHAPTER 9

Caro's hands trembled as she awaited Gavin. She had performed every task she could as she counted the minutes until he would arrive at her room. Industriousness had distracted her as she took down her hair and brushed it, as she stepped out of her scandalous gown and tight stays, and as she slipped into a far more comfortable night rail with a dressing gown atop the entire affair. She had tidied the books on the bedside table. Had paced the carpet at least three dozen times. Had studied her reflection in the looking glass and draped all her hair over her left shoulder, then her right shoulder, and then she had heaved a sigh and sent it all cascading down her back.

Now, she was back to pacing the length of the chamber once more, wondering when he would arrive. And wondering whether or not she would go mad before he would appear. They had parted ways after their meeting with Jasper, and her heart was still overwhelmed with the manner in which he had championed her.

Her warrior had faced Lord Derby, and he had also faced Jasper. Not many men would have been brave enough to do so. How she admired him. He was kind and true and good, Gavin Winter. Her love for him was growing stronger by the day, and she knew without a doubt she would need to speak with Jasper in the morning, regardless of what happened between herself and Gavin tonight.

He deserved to know the truth, and she could no longer bear the burden of keeping it from him. Her promise to Jasper would have to be broken. Her love for Gavin came first.

A gentle tap sounded on the door, and she went racing across her chamber, stopping and passing a quick hand over her riotous hair before she opened the door. He smiled when he saw her, and God's teeth, he was handsome when he smiled.

She rose on her toes and cast a furtive glance down the hall behind him to make certain no one was about. "Come in," she whispered.

His grin deepened as he crossed the threshold, the door closing at his back. "Why are we whispering?"

She chuckled at his question, which had been asked in a soft undertone. "I do not know. No doubt you think me silly, fretting over you being here."

"I took great care, Caro. No one will know save us, but if you want me to go, I will."

"No!" The vehemence of her response took the both of them by surprise, if his countenance was any indication.

He winked. Oh, he was a charmer and a rogue.

How she loved him.

"I'll stay then, as long as you haven't forgotten your promise?"

She had told him she would sing for him. A sudden rush of shyness hit her as she shook her head. "I have not forgotten. However, I do hope I won't hurt your ears."

"Never. The sound of your voice is the loveliest thing I

have ever heard." His eyes took on a glint as they swept over her.

She wondered if she should have donned another gown instead of the robe and night rail she wore. While modest, the combination was far more intimate than one of her work gowns would have been. She thrust the worry from her mind, for it was too late to change her dress. He was here, just where she wanted him, and that mattered more than anything else.

"Come and have a seat," she said. "You ought to be comfortable, at least, if you must listen to me warble."

Gamely, Gavin allowed her to take his good hand in hers and guide him to the chair positioned before her looking glass.

"As you wish it, but there is no *must* about listening to you sing. It is what I desire more than anything else. Well, it is what I desire that I can actually *have* this evening." He dutifully sat.

She stood before him, those words of his tucking into her heart and sending heat blossoming between her thighs. A wicked urge bloomed.

You can have me, too, she wanted to say.

But that would be far too bold, and she had no wish for him to think her too common or forward. She wanted to impress him tonight. Because it may very well be the last they would share together after she confessed the truth to him on the morrow.

"I've never sung for a man like this before," she admitted.

She had sung for her family in the past and for the patrons of The Sinner's Palace. She had not sung for Philip, and never for a man whom she loved. Gavin was the only one. She knew with an aching, devastating certainty that he always would be.

The smile he gave her was tender. "I am honored to be the first treated to such a performance."

She took a deep, fortifying breath, and felt a quiver of trepidation roll through her. Could she sing to him thus? It was such an intimate act. When she sang before the patrons, she often settled her gaze upon the wall or the ceiling; sometimes, she closed her eyes. But with Gavin, there was nowhere else she wanted to look.

All she wanted to see was him, to forever imprint the memory of this night, and the way he was gazing at her with undisguised adoration, upon her mind.

Holding his stare, she began to sing the lyrics of Dibdin's *The Soldier's Adieu*. "Adieu, adieu my only life. My honor calls me from thee…" The nervousness subsided, her confidence growing as she warmed to the haunting melody and words. "When on the wings of thy dear love to heaven above…" And as she reached the final chorus, she softened her voice, allowing the sadness of the ditty to cloak her heart. "…shall call a guardian angel down to watch me in the battle."

Gavin rose to his feet and took her in his arms at once. "My God, Caro, that was even more beautiful than I supposed. You've the voice of an angel."

She linked her arms around his neck, breathing in the familiar scent of him, shaving soap and musky man. He was so warm, so vibrant, so strong. It was difficult indeed to reconcile the Gavin Winter in her arms to the beast of a man who was England's most renowned prizefighter. He was such a gentle man, so tender and sweet.

What would happen when he regained his memory? Would he take up prizefighting once more? Would he hate her for keeping the truth from him?

She hoped not.

"I do not have the voice of an angel, but I thank you for

saying so," she told him, trying to keep her own sorrows at bay.

"You are unhappy," he observed, frowning down at her. "Why? Was it the song? Are you thinking of what happened earlier?"

It was a combination of everything, she supposed, but the most pressing matter of all was the secret she withheld. The more time they spent together, the greater the betrayal she committed.

She bit her lip, tamping down those emotions. She would worry about the truth tomorrow. Tonight, she wanted to give him the truest part of herself, the part which she had never given another.

"I am not unhappy," she denied. "It is the song, I think. The thought of soldiers going off to war, never to return. So many good men have been lost to battle."

"I wonder…" His brow furrowed and he paused, his words trailing off. "Perhaps I was a soldier, and that is why I am plagued by these memories of violence."

Tell him, Caro.

Tell him now.

But she was selfish, and she could not find the words that would undoubtedly end them. "Your memories will return to you soon," she said with a certainty she did not possess.

In truth, her knowledge of such cases as his was severely limited. She had been poring over the few medical treatises she had been able to find, and the truth was, Gavin may never regain his memory on his own. But others who knew him could help him in trying to spur the memories.

Likely, he needed that now, while the wound to his head was still relatively fresh. All the more reason to tell him.

"Even if they do not return," he said softly, his palms gliding up and down the small of her back and drawing her body flusher to his, "I do not need them. All I need is you."

How she hoped he would feel the same after he discovered what she had done.

"I need you too," she told him, meaning those words. "Will you stay here with me tonight?"

"Caro," he growled, then lowered his head to press his forehead to hers. "You ask too much of me. I cannot stay in this room with you without making love to you."

"Good, because that is what I want."

He tensed. "We aren't yet wed."

We may never be.

The reminder was like ice being dumped on all the warmth burning to life within her.

"I do not care," she returned. "That will come in time. Please. I need you. After everything that happened today, I want to forget. I want to be wrapped in your arms and your strength, and I want to *know* you."

"Damn it, woman. You sing like an angel and heal like a witch, flit around like a butterfly, and call to me like a bloody siren." He raised his head, searching her gaze. "Which one is the true Caroline Sutton, I wonder? Each of them?"

"The true Caroline Sutton is the one who loves you."

He groaned. "This isn't fair to you, love. I don't even know who I am."

But I know who you are.

She wet her lips, guilt gnawing at her. "I do not care who you are, aside from the man I see standing before me. Who you were before is immaterial."

"What if I ain't the sort of man you would love?" he asked. "What if I remember everything and I'm a monster? A criminal? What if I'm a vile swine like that fancy nob who was accosting you tonight?"

"Hush." She pressed a finger to his lips. "What if you are none of those things, and all your worrying is for naught? What if you kiss me and allow your worries to slip away?"

He kissed the pad of her finger, then plucked it away from his mouth. "What if I kiss you and I never want to stop?"

"That sounds like heaven to me."

"Damn. It does to me, too." He sighed, pinning her with his vibrant-emerald stare. "I did not come to you tonight for this. Especially after what happened in the hell with that bastard of a viscount."

"Pray do not mention him now. I don't want to think about that."

"Fair enough. We shan't. But, Caro, you must know how it feels, coming to you after what I saw." His gaze was open, earnest. *Loving*. "I would never wish for you to regret your decision. If you're making it in haste—"

"I am not," she interrupted. "What is between us has no relation to what occurred earlier. You are not that sort of man. You are a true gentleman. Noble, loyal, brave, sweet, and true. You could not be more different from Derby."

"You are sure?"

His hold on her tightened, his eyes searching hers. "I've never been more certain of anything."

He gave a jerky nod, his expression turning adorably shy. "If we are to... If we... Hell, Caro. I don't know how to go about this. Or mayhap I do. The trouble is, I don't recall. The man I am now has no notion of what comes next."

She smiled, drinking in the sight of him, flushing and embarrassed and beloved in her arms, this tall, hulking beast of a man. Her gentle giant. Her love.

"I have no notion of what comes next either," she admitted. She had allowed Philip liberties, but she had never lain with him, and she was more grateful than ever for her restraint now.

Because she wanted to experience lovemaking for the

first time with Gavin Winter and no one else. Even if he did not remember who he was.

He inhaled slowly, his hands traveling in the same, delicious caress up and down her back. His head dipped toward hers. "The way you look at me...I could never tire of that. You wear your heart for me to see."

She smiled, but his words filled her with sadness, too. And more guilt. Just like the song she had sung for him, which had been a soldier's hopeful belief his love's prayers would keep him safe in battle, Gavin seemed to believe her an angel.

How wrong he was. And how deeply she hated herself. But not enough to stop.

"I love you," she told him, because that, at least, was truth.

"I love you, Caro." His head dipped, and his mouth crushed hers in a passionate, claiming kiss.

* * *

THEY HAD KISSED their way to Caro's bed, stripped each other of their garments, and settled in it together, bodies entwined, her softness against his hardness. He was acutely aware of his size compared to hers—she felt so small and precious in his arms, and he had no wish to crush her beneath his massive body.

It occurred to him that while his body knew what it wanted, his mind was uncertain of the steps. Was he a bloody virgin? He had no inkling. It hardly mattered, aside from his desire to make Caro weep with bliss.

He wanted to lick her until she screamed and came on his tongue.

That hardly seemed the thought of an inexperienced man, did it?

He deepened their kiss, his tongue teasing hers, as he gave

in to his weakness and passed a hand down the smooth roundness of her belly to the apex of her thighs. She was hot and silken. He dared to explore lower, parting her folds until he found her slick and smooth. The plump bud of her sex greeted his fingers, and he swirled over it in a gentle massage, testing her, learning what she liked.

Everything was new. Himself, the woman in his arms, this love. He felt as if the heavens had opened and unimaginable gifts had been showered upon him. Hell, if this was the reward for nearly cocking up his toes behind an East End gaming hell, he would gladly suffer all the pain and punishment again just to have this moment.

Just to have this woman.

To have his Caro.

He increased the pressure on her nubbin, and her hips bucked. She made a low, seductive sound that he swallowed with his kiss. So ready, his sweet Caro. So wet. *Fuck*, his cock was hard as iron, pressed against the softness of her belly. His ballocks were drawn taut with need. It had been too long —he knew not how long—since he had found true release beyond the comfort his hand could provide.

But he told himself he would not rush their coupling. He wanted to savor her. To seduce her. To give her as much pleasure as he possibly could. He tore his mouth from hers and dragged kisses down her throat, all while his fingers continued plying their torture, fast and hard until she made the most delicious sounds deep in her throat, then slow and soft pets that had her clutching at him and pleading for more.

Oh, how sweet she was.

He kissed down the velvet softness of her chest, stopping when he reached the silken patch of skin between the swells of her breasts. He withdrew his fingers from her cunny so he could leverage himself on his uninjured arm, free of pain, and kissed the perfect roundness of her breast. Her nipple was pink and perfect, hard and calling to him, begging for his mouth. He sucked the stiff peak, then swirled his tongue over her, and she moaned, rocking beneath him.

His.

He nipped her lightly, the ferocity of his need making him catch her hungry nipple between his teeth and tug until she moaned, her fingers threading through his hair and her back bowing from the bed. He tormented the both of them a bit more before raising his head to drink in the sight of her, naked and flushed and wanting. She presented a delectable offering, all smooth skin and beautiful curves, pink and feminine and so beautiful, she made his cock weep.

But this was only the beginning.

There was more he wanted.

So much more.

He dragged his lips down her stomach, all the way to the heart of her. When her thighs parted, revealing her pink, glistening depths to him, a bolt of desire so potent that he nearly unmanned himself right then slammed into him. He bowed his head, opened her folds, and sucked her pearl.

She cried out, bucking against him. She was musky and sweet on his tongue, and he took his time devouring her with slow, long licks. Listening to the sensual sounds she made—her mewls and gasps and hitches of breath—he drove them both into a frenzy.

When she reached her pinnacle, crying out as she shuddered beneath him, he knew he could not maintain his restraint for much longer. He rose over her, careful to leverage his body on his good arm, and rolled his hips against hers. Teasing, testing.

She was so slick, his cock glanced over her folds, sending desire roaring through him. The need to be inside her consumed him, and in that moment, he swore he would forego air just to join his body to hers. Rubbing the head of his prick over her seam, he took in her loveliness. Her auburn hair was wild on the pillow, framing her face in a tangle of luxurious curls. Her lips were parted, her skin flushed, eyes almost gray.

"Caro, my darling, my love." The words were torn from him, his heart pounding fast, his body aflame. "I've never seen a more beautiful sight than you naked beneath me."

"Make me yours," she murmured, reaching for him, careful to avoid the scarred yet healing flesh that still pained him.

Her caress traveled over his shoulders, down his arms, over his chest. He could not resist dipping his head and taking her mouth. She kissed him with wild abandon, dragging him nearer to the edge, closer to losing control.

He sucked on the fullness of her lower lip before raising his head. "Are you ready for me, darling? I can't wait."

"Always."

Gripping his cock, he guided himself to her entrance. It was strange how he had forgotten so much of himself, but this, making love to Caro, was elemental. Natural, easy, *right*.

Perfection.

In the dim corners of his mind, he recalled a woman's first time could cause her pain. Though how he knew that, he could not say.

Slowly, he told himself. *Gently.*

He allowed himself a shallow thrust, then paused as she stiffened beneath him. She was incredibly tight, and he was trapped in her slick heat, but not nearly as deep as he wanted —needed—to be.

He kissed her tenderly, then toyed with the responsive bud of her sex, gratified at her sigh of pleasure. She moved beneath him, hips tipping upward, seeking. He broke the kiss as white-hot desire shot down his spine.

"How are you, love? Shall I go on?" he asked, his voice thick with lust.

"If you don't go on, I'll die," she murmured.

He grinned, her words taking him by surprise. "We can't have that happen, can we?"

He moved again, thrusting deeper. She clamped on him, her body undulating against his, spurring him on. The tension in her began to fade as he swirled tantalizing circles over her nub. Wetness urged him deeper.

Her fingers dug into the muscles of his shoulders. He kissed her again as he finally seated himself deep. Her drenched cunny around him was the most glorious sensation he had ever experienced. Tentatively, he began a rhythm, sliding in and out of her, making certain to continue torturing her pearl and break their kisses to suckle her nipples.

When she seized on him, her body stiffening as another release claimed her, she moaned. He swallowed the sound with his kiss and groaned into her mouth as he moved faster, deeper, harder, spurred on by the way her channel milked his cock. Another instinct rose in him, reminding him he needed to avoid spending within her. But the sensation was too divine, and it had been far too long since he had experienced such pleasure.

His ballocks tightened, and he exploded, his seed pouring from him, filling her before he could withdraw. The rush of bliss showered over him like sparks from a raging fire. Hot, beyond control, dangerous.

In the dizzying wake of their union, he collapsed against her, pressing a kiss to her shoulder. He felt as if he had just found the part of himself that had been missing. The emotions buzzing through him were incredible, unlike any he had experienced since waking up without a memory. He felt...whole.

How fortunate he was to have found his way to Caro, his own guardian angel. He did not think he had ever experienced such happiness, such a feeling of belonging, as if he were doing exactly what he was meant to do. Mayhap their meeting had been preordained. It certainly felt as if a higher power had guided them together.

"I love you, butterfly," he said. "I love you so bloody much."

Her hands were everywhere, gentle and tender, caressing his back, cupping his face. "I love you too."

"Thank you for tonight," he said, stroking her hair as he gazed at her lovely face. "Thank you for finding me, for healing me, for making me whole."

"Oh, my darling man," she whispered, shadows passing in her eyes for a moment before they were gone, "it is I who must be grateful to you. You owe me nothing."

"I owe you everything, Caro." He kissed her lingeringly, until they were both breathless, and his heart was alive with the endless possibility of the love blossoming between them. "But for now, all I have to offer you is my heart."

CHAPTER 10

*H*e woke to sunlight.

To a warm, feminine form curled against him.

To the sweet, floral scent of Caro Sutton teasing his senses.

And memories.

He woke to his *name.*

Gavin Winter.

And that was it. After so many weeks of wondering, of agonizing, of scouring his mind for something more than the mists inhabiting it since he had been beaten and shot and left for dead, his answers returned to him. The flow of remembrance was slow at first. His siblings—Gen, Demon, Devil, Dom, Blade, Dev, Bea, Grace, Pru, Eugie, and Christabella. The interior of the rooms he kept—spare and small, nothing but a bed and a place to shave in a seedy part of the rookery where a chap would as soon pick your pocket as bid you good day.

Then more. His favorite food: pigeon pie with lemon pudding for dessert. His favorite poison: arrack. And hell, the nights he had recently spent with his brother Demon, drinking himself to oblivion in preparation for his fight…

Fight.

His hands flexed into fists.

He was a prizefighter.

Suddenly, all the flashes of violence, the understanding of what it felt like to hit a man—he understood them. He had spent the last few years of his life building his reputation as one of the best damned prizefighters in London. And his body had taken a beating over those years.

Worse, cumulatively, than the beating he had received…

As remembrance rained down on him, like a sudden storm on a clear day, he found himself immobile, stiffer than a statue in Caro's bed. Searing pain, the likes of which he had not suffered since the early days of his recovery, shot through his head. It was almost as if the memories were too much, too fast, rushing at him, arsey varsey.

He clutched his head in his hands, closing his eyes tight against the sunlight, but the memories kept coming. He remembered being surrounded by men. Five of them. Defending himself as best he could, but he had been outnumbered. Just flashes of remembrance, this. But he recalled the crack of the pistol, the crash of something over his skull, the darkness that had claimed him. The faces of the bastards responsible remained indistinct.

Fucking hell.

Had he known them? Who had attacked him, and why?

A moan tore from him as his head continued to ache. Slowly, he became aware of something beyond his inner torment. Of a soothing hand on his brow, of a soft, dulcet voice laced with concern.

"What is the matter? Are you unwell?"

Gavin struggled to form words, but the overwhelming return of his memories seemed to have rendered his tongue numb. Or mayhap the connection from his knowledge box to his mouth had been severed. Whatever the case, he could not speak.

Could scarcely manage to turn his head and meet her beloved hazel gaze.

Beloved.

Bloody hell.

He had fallen in love with a Sutton. With Caro Sutton. Their families had been enemies for far longer than they had been in a reluctant truce.

Once more, he tried to speak, but there was nothing. No words. Words were filling his head, however, and so was concern. None of this made sense. How had he ended up in the alleyway behind The Sinner's Palace? He had not been going there, had he? Gavin didn't give a damn about gaming, and if he wished it, he could always scratch that itch at his own family's hell, The Devil's Spawn.

Caro's expressive face showed her concern. "Can you not say anything, darling?"

He shook his head.

"Water?" she asked.

Aye, maybe that would help. But what he truly required was arrack. A whole damned bottle of it, poured straight down his gullet. That way, he could dull the pain and chase the memories until he was ready to confront them.

There was a rush of movement as she left the bed. Had he not been in utter agony, he would have admired her curves, her waist, all that glossy auburn hair cascading down her back to brush the perfect handfuls of her rump. But he was in misery, so all he could do was stare and hope the water would loosen his tongue and mind both.

She was at his side in a breeze of cool morning air, holding a cup to his lips. He allowed her to tend him as she had done when he had been an invalid. It was an eerie echo of the last time he had awoken from a deep sleep to find Caro Sutton at his side. He drank greedily, his mouth somehow drier than it had ever been.

At least swallowing was an action he was capable of performing.

When he'd had his fill, she withdrew the cup. "Enough?"

"Aye," he managed past a throat that felt thick and unused.

But that wasn't true, was it? He had spoken plenty in the last few weeks when he had been a man with no name and no past. It was somehow the oddness of speaking as Gavin for the first time in so long, coupled with the ache in his head, that had rendered him badly shaken.

"Speak to me, my love," she coaxed gently, perching on the bed beside him.

She was completely naked. Even in his strange state, he could not keep his eyes from her bare breasts and pretty pink nipples, hardened by the chill in the air. He recalled in exquisite detail just how much she liked it when he sucked them.

The buoyancy in his chest was sudden and strange. He felt as if he were inhaling fresh breath, new life. As if he were reborn. The man he had been before and the man he was now joined.

"I remember," he said, dragging his gaze to her wide hazel eyes. "I know who I am."

"You remember?" The cup in her hands fell to the floor with a dull thud, sending the rest of the water spilling across the carpet.

Neither of them paid it much heed.

He was too fixated upon her, upon the memories returning to him, the odd change overtaking his body and mind. He wanted to smile, but could not. Was it the pain of remembrance? Or was the return of so much information at once too damned much for his mind to bear?

He couldn't be sure. "I remember everything except what happened the night I was wounded. It's the devil of a thing, but I woke with my name in my mind. And as I saw the sunlight, it all came rushing over me like a flood."

"This is wonderful," she said, but she did not smile.

Nor did she seem particularly happy to hear he once more had memories and an identity. Was it because she feared he would change his mind now that he knew who he was?

"This changes nothing for us, Caro," he said softly.

Which was a lie. He was a Winter; she was a Sutton. Uniting their families would be damned difficult. But remembering he was Gavin Winter had done nothing to dim the love he felt for her. He would do anything necessary to make Caro his wife.

She worried her lip, her fingers plucking at the counterpane which had fallen around his waist. "Surely it will change some things."

"Not the important things." He grinned despite the throbbing in his skull.

He was so damned happy. Relieved. *Hell.* His family must have been worried about him. Had they believed him dead? There was so much he needed to discover. He had to make his way to them as soon as he could, to let them know he was alive.

"Gavin," she said, her countenance ashen, "there is something I must tell you."

He noticed her use of his name. And how odd it was, hearing it on her lips. Of recognizing it, of the feeling of belonging that went along with it. He was Gavin Winter, and how right it felt to finally know who he was. To have a name, a past, a memory, a family, a purpose. He had returned to himself.

Thank God.

But Caro…

There was something about her use of his name which rang false. Which seemed inherently wrong. His befuddled mind could not quite place it or make sense of what was happening even as his instincts seemed to. His gut clenched and a cold sweat erupted on his brow. He was hot and cold at once, the room spinning about him.

Hell, he was going to be ill.

"Chamber pot," he ground out, knowing he did not have much time.

She fetched it for him, pressing the cold porcelain into his hands as the contents of his stomach rebelled.

He heaved into the vessel, misery mingling with the pain in his head. His whole mind felt as if it were falling apart, like a carriage which had gone off a cliff and been smashed to bits.

She took the chamber pot away as his stomach calmed, but in the wake of casting up his accounts, his jumbled mind understood his body's violent reaction.

He had yet to tell her his name, and she had called him *Gavin*.

"How did you know my name?" he demanded, fists clenching in the bedclothes as the room continued to swim around him. "I haven't told you, Caro."

She blanched, then broke his gaze, glancing down at her nudity before rushing to find her discarded night rail. The one he had removed from her with such profound longing last night.

Last night, when everything had been different.

Last night, when everything had been a bloody fucking *lie*.

He could not remain in her bed for one moment longer. Not when the devastating blow of realization hit him with the force of any bareknuckle fist. All these weeks of believing her an angel, of allowing himself to fall in love with her...

"How long have you known?" he growled, slipping from the bed, uncaring of his nudity.

He was a wild man now. Needing to know the truth. Sick at the notion of what it would bring, what it would mean. He forgot about his aching head as he found his trousers and angrily jammed his legs into them.

She was flitting about, pacing the small chamber, her bare feet flying over the carpet, her face a study in worry. His butterfly was still flitting, but now he did not find her nearly as entrancing as he once had.

He needed the truth.

She owed him that much.

"Damn it, Caro, say something." His words were hoarse with torment as he fastened his trousers and stalked toward her, bare-chested. "Speak to me."

She remained rooted to the spot, watching him with wide, shocked eyes as he stormed to her, stopping near enough that her exotic scent hit him. The scent of betrayal.

"Gavin, please calm yourself. I fear for your health, for your mind. It cannot be good for you to be so angry while you are recovering."

"Ha!" His laughter was bitter. He wanted to reach for her, wanted to kiss her cruelly. To make her tell him the words he didn't want to hear but knew he must. "Do not, I beg you, feign concern over me now. You'll pardon me if I doubt the sincerity."

"I do care," she said, reaching for him. "I love you, Gavin."

He shrugged away from her touch, wanting no part of it. "Don't speak to me of love. Not until you tell me the truth. How long have you been deceiving me?"

Her lip trembled, her hazel eyes filling with unshed tears. "I have known from the moment Jasper recognized you."

"And when the hell was that?" he spat, growing weary of playing games with her.

Sutton to the core, this one. How had he ever believed her to be sweet and good and true?

"Before you woke," she admitted.

He had been expecting the blow. He had suspected. Gavin Winter was not a fool. At least, he had not been one before he had lost his memory. But his memory had returned to him, and with it, his sanity. He would no longer be kept a prisoner by the Suttons. He would have his freedom this day, damn it. But though he had anticipated the truth—her countenance and reaction to his questions had told him all he needed to know—he had not been prepared for how much it would hurt.

He had faced masterful opponents as a prizefighter. Had received any number of powerful fists to the jaw, to the head, to the bread basket. *Hell*, he had been beaten near to death not long ago. But nothing—not one whit of any of those beatings—held a candle to the pain he felt now.

Because this was a pain which would not heal. It came from within. From his stupid, trusting, wretched heart.

"You have known who I am," he managed to say, "all these weeks. As I have shared with you my struggle to recall the simplest details of my life, as I have trusted you and grown to care for the woman I mistakenly thought you to be, you have been deceiving me."

Her face crumpled, and the tears fell in truth, streaming down her pale cheeks. "Yes, but it is not what you think. I wanted to tell you—"

"You *wanted* to tell me?" He unleashed a bitter bark of laughter, his lips twisting into a sneer. "If you had wanted to tell me, you would have done. Instead, you allowed me to wallow in this state of half living, not knowing who I am or where I belong. You lured me into your bed, made me believe myself in love with you. And still, you never spoke the five words which would have changed everything for me."

"Gavin, please—"

"*I know who you are*," he roared, cutting her off once more. "Those were the bloody words, Caroline Sutton. The ones you should have spoken to me instead of all the lies you fed me."

She. Had. Known.

It was all he could think.

And he was devastated. Ruined. Rocked to his core. Last night, he had fallen asleep thinking himself the most fortunate man in the world, and this morning, he had opened his eyes to a goddamn nightmare.

"I…" She paused, pressing a hand to her lips to stifle a sob before continuing. "You are right. I should have told you. But I was duty-bound to keep the secret. My brother had asked it of me, and I believed I was protecting you by doing so."

"Protecting me?" His head was throbbing with a new vengeance.

"Yes, protecting you," she said. "There is someone in the world who wanted you dead, and forgive me for believing it was better to let that someone suppose you were."

He shook his head, wishing the action would clear the pain confusing his mind, his heart, his very soul. "I don't believe anything you say. You're a Sutton and a liar, and I wish to God you had let me die in that fucking street."

She gasped. "You don't mean that, Gavin."

"Aye," he told her ruthlessly. "I do. I would have been better off."

Without bothering to collect the remainder of his garments, and without having a care over whether anyone would see him leaving her room half-nude in the early hours of the morning, he spun on his heel and left.

He was going back to where he belonged: the Winter family.

* * *

CARO RUSHED to don a chemise and gown, not bothering with stays, and bound her hair hastily in a simple braid with shaking fingers. Her heart was in agony, her stomach in knots, and her mouth had gone dry. Gavin had been furious when he had discovered the truth, and she could not blame him for his reaction to her deception. But she was desperate to find him and try to explain before she lost him forever.

If she had not already done so. *Merciful saints.*

Without bothering to put on slippers, she raced from her room, then down the narrow stairs to the floor housing most of the private rooms. Gavin was nowhere in sight, heightening her panic.

What would he do if anyone tried to keep him from leaving? What if he left before she could catch him and try to speak with him? Where would he go?

The questions were rushing through her mind faster than her traveling feet when she turned a corner and collided with her brother.

Jasper caught her, steadying her, his expression concerned. "Christ, Caro. You can't go bolting about the halls."

His voice was annoyed but not alarmed, and it occurred to her that the hour was terribly early for him to be awake. Unless he had not gone to sleep, which would hardly have been surprising, knowing her brother.

Barnaby, one of Jasper's dogs, was at his side, and the canine let out a loud bark that sounded remarkably similar to an admonition.

She tried to collect her thoughts, but her desperation was rising. "I need to find Gavin. Have you seen him?"

Her brother scowled. "Why would you have need to find him at this time of the morning, sister? What the devil is that mark on your swallow?"

Her hand crept to her throat. *Oh, bloody blue blazes.* This was not the conversation she wanted to be having now.

Or ever.

"Never mind that. I need to speak with him." She attempted to wrest herself from her brother's hold, but he was not having it.

Jasper frowned. "Why, I asked you? Speak or I'll tell Barnaby to rip off his ear."

Barnaby barked, but Caro knew the dog was nowhere near as ferocious as her brother pretended or as he looked. Quite the opposite, in fact. Barnaby was a big, sweet, slobbering darling. But not even her fondness for her brother's beloved dog could shake her from the worry and the fear threatening to overtake her.

The truth fled her.

"He *knows*, Jasper."

She didn't need to elaborate.

Her brother stiffened. "Sodding hell. When?"

"This morning," she explained, well aware of the conclusions her brother would draw from the admission.

Correct conclusions, as it happened.

But she would fret over that later. For now, her primary concern lay elsewhere. Namely, in the man who had told her he had wished she had left him to die rather than to save him. The man she had fallen in love with over the course of the last few weeks. The man she had given herself to.

"Morning," Jasper growled grimly, his jaw hardening. "The sun has scarcely risen, Caro. What the hell were you doing with him at this hour?"

She swallowed. "I..."

Before she could explain, a roar interrupted her words. "Sutton!"

Gavin was stalking toward them, face contorted with fury, and though he now wore a shirt along with yesterday's trousers, he looked rumpled and disreputable. She had never seen him look so dangerous.

Barnaby barked.

"Call off your dog and face me like a man, Sutton," Gavin growled.

Jasper released his hold on Caro and turned to square off with Gavin. "Sit, Barnaby," he ordered his dog.

Barnaby sat very near to her brother's booted feet, eying Gavin as warily as Caro and Jasper undoubtedly were. Her heart lurched at the pain in his handsome face. She had caused it. She was partly to blame. Could he ever forgive her?

"Gavin," she said, trying to go to him.

Jasper shot out a staying hand, keeping her beside himself and Barnaby. "Stay where you are, Caro. Winter 'ere's got some questions that need answering if he doesn't want me to send him back to 'is troublesome family in pieces. Why the 'ell were you in my sister's room this morning?"

Caro noted that her brother was dropping the *h* from some of his words once more, a sure sign he was disgruntled. And the rage emanating from Gavin was palpable. He was pale, fists clenched at his sides, his glare pinned upon Jasper. No good could come of a clash between these two men who were both so beloved to her.

"Gavin," she tried again, her voice pleading. "Look at me."

"No," he denied, refusing her entreaty.

Her heart was breaking. After the tenderness of the night before, to wake to this nightmare was devastating.

"Please," she begged.

"Get out of my sight, Caro," he spat. "This is between myself and your bastard of a brother."

"Careful who you're insulting, Winter," Jasper warned, his voice silken with menace. "You have much to answer for too, don't you? Why were you with my sister this morning?"

Gavin's lip curled. "Ask her."

Barnaby barked once more. He was an unusually smart dog, and he did not like conflict of any sort, which had oft proven a boon when it came to rising tempers in the gaming hell. Barnaby spotted problem patrons before their voices were sufficiently raised and they were challenging each other to name their seconds.

Caro patted the dog's soft head, trying to calm him.

"I asked you," Jasper returned.

"And I don't owe you an explanation." Gavin's fists were still clenched. "You've been keeping me a prisoner in this miserable hell for weeks, and all this time, you've known who I am but kept it a secret from me. Why?"

Jasper shrugged. "Why not?"

His taunting reply propelled Gavin forward.

The two men collided, fists flying, as Caro clung to a barking Barnaby and watched the mayhem unfolding. "Gavin, Jasper, please stop this!" she cried out, terrified that they would injure each other.

That Jasper would land a blow that would send Gavin spiraling back into the abyss, where he had no memories and no name. Or that Gavin's prizefighting instincts would have him thrashing Jasper. But neither of them listened to her entreaties. They fought on, landing blows, grunting, as their punches escalated into a war.

The commotion brought some of the guards racing down the hall, and it required the efforts of Randall, Hugh, and Bennet to force the two men apart. Her brothers Rafe and Hart appeared as well, aiding in holding Jasper back. Caro sobbed into Barnaby's fur at the sight before her—bloodied, bruised faces, so much anger.

Her fault, all of it.

"Take him to The Devil's Spawn," Jasper spat around a mouthful of blood. "I want him gone."

"That makes two of us," Gavin sneered.

The glance he cast in Caro's direction—at long last—was venomous. He said nothing to her, simply curled his lip, and turned his back on her.

What had she done?

CHAPTER 11

Caro hovered at the threshold of her chamber—the room Gavin had spent the last few weeks inhabiting. Everything was as he had left it, but the room was empty and lifeless and still. On the floor, there were some broken bits of crockery she did not have the heart to sweep up. In all, it was a perfect reflection of what she felt within.

He was gone.

He had left without saying goodbye. Without giving her the opportunity to explain her part in the deception. Not that she was certain an explanation would change his mind. Quite likely, the betrayal she had committed was unforgivable.

She had known better, of course. But she had been torn between her brother and a man who had initially been a stranger to her. A man who had become so much more over the course of the time she had perpetuated the secret. Each day that had passed had brought her closer to the certain knowledge that she must reveal everything to him.

And she had meant to. She had promised herself last

night that she was going to tell him everything this morning, regardless of her promise to Jasper.

But he had risen with memories returning to him, and she had been hopeful and terrified all at once. Hopeful that he would no longer suffer the pain of a mind free of memories and of not knowing who he was. Terrified that when he discovered her complicity in keeping his identity from him, he would never want to speak to her again.

She had not been wrong in that fear.

"What are you doing, sister?" asked a familiar voice.

Not the one she wanted to hear.

She turned to find Jasper approaching her, disappointment etched in his expression and tone. The blood on his face had been wiped clean, but his right eye was bruised and swelling. She winced as she took in the evidence of that morning's terrible debacle.

"You are wanting to speak with me, I suppose," she returned, her stomach twisting again at the thought.

"You owe me an explanation, and I owe you one as well," he said cryptically. "Come and take some wine with me, and we'll patter."

"I don't want to speak now," she said, feeling mulish. "Can it not wait?"

"No." Jasper was somber. "It can't. Wine and patter or I lock you in this room until you squeak."

Ah, he wanted her confession. She had known he would, after she had revealed Gavin had been in her room this morning and he had seen the evidence of their night of passion on her throat. Sad evidence. All she had left of Gavin, it would seem, and not nearly enough. She may have deceived him these last few weeks, but doing so had been against her will. She had never lied about her love for him.

"Wine and patter it is," she conceded sadly, hating herself for what she had done. Hating herself for losing Gavin.

"Good choice." Jasper offered her his arm like a fancy cove, the effect somewhat comical with his swollen eye.

But she took his arm just the same and allowed him to lead her to his office. Barnaby had been sleeping by Jasper's desk, snoring like a drunken sailor. As they crossed the threshold, he woke, yawned, and rose to greet them. To Caro, he offered a sniff and a lick of her hand, as if to tell her he remembered what had happened several hours before. She scratched the dog's head and swallowed down a lump rising in her throat.

"Too soft, this hound of mine," Jasper muttered, shaking his head as he crossed to the sideboard where he kept an array of spirits.

"He is a sweet lad," Caro said, gazing into Barnaby's wide, brown eyes.

Barnaby sneezed, then made a whining sound before sitting on her feet.

"He's worried about you," Jasper observed, pouring them some wine and returning to her, holding out a glass in offering. "He ain't the only one."

"I am perfectly fine," she lied, then raised the Madeira to her lips, swallowing the cool, rich liquid and wishing it could wash away her pain.

"You're swilling your wine like a toss pot."

So she was. But damn him for noticing.

This mess was all his making, curse it.

Her anger toward him and his forced secrets returned, replacing the sadness. "This is all your bloody fault, Jasper. If you had allowed me to tell him who he was weeks ago, he never would have found out in this way."

Jasper raised his glass in a mocking salute. "I was meant to be the fucking hero of this tale, believe it or not. One bloody favor, and have a look at what happens. A ham-fisted

Winter puppy blackens my eye after he's been bedding my sister."

She winced at the anger in her brother's voice. "He hasn't been bedding me, and he's hardly a puppy."

"Acts like one, and if he ain't bedding you, how'd you get that love bite on your damned neck, and what was he doing with you this morning?"

She drank some more wine, delaying the inevitable. "It was one night only."

Her cheeks were on fire. Never had she imagined having to engage in such a discussion with her brother. Her utter mortification was complete.

"Satan's teeth," Jasper growled. "They're going to pay for this, the lot of them."

"Please do not strike up another war with the Winters over what happened between myself and Gavin," she begged, despising the thought.

Suttons and Winters had been competitors and mortal enemies for years until recent developments and the need to work together had forced them to find common ground. She had no wish to be the cause of a return to hostilities.

"No." Her brother shook his head, his jaw going hard. "Nothing you say will change what needs to be done. They are the reason I kept him under this roof for so long. They are the ones who asked me to keep his presence here quiet. This is how I am repaid for going to them the moment I discovered you had found Gavin Winter's sorry arse in the alley."

She frowned at her brother, confusion settling over her. "You went to the Winters and told them we'd found Gavin?"

"Aye. More fool I am." Jasper raked his fingers through his dark hair, then drained the last of his wine. "I should have demanded a ransom. Instead, like a bloody dupe, I agreed to their plan."

Her heart was pounding harder now, her mind beginning to make sense of her brother's furious rants. "What was their plan?"

"To keep 'im here until they could get to the bottom of who'd tried to crash 'im."

In his outrage, Jasper was once more dropping the *h* and speaking flash. "They knew for certain that someone was trying to kill him? That what happened to Gavin was not the work of footpads or some other bad sort?"

"Aye. Apparently another of the Winters, Demon, took a lick on the head not long before Gavin nearly cocked up his toes."

Icy fear laced through her heart. She had suspected as much, but somehow, hearing Jasper give credence to her suspicions made the idea of someone attempting to kill Gavin far more real than it had been before. And now, he was no longer protected. No one had known he was alive, but soon, everyone would. Including the person or people who wanted him dead.

"Why did you not tell me the truth?" she demanded. "You never spoke a word of this before. If I had known—"

"If you had known," Jasper interrupted, "it may have put you in danger as well. Or any of the rest of us. I did what I thought best, and so did they."

"You made me lie to him," she shouted.

Barnaby rose from his place on her feet and made an agitated turn about the room.

"If you'd told 'im who he was, he'd have gone back to The Devil's Spawn, and what good would it have done 'im?" he countered.

And he was so calm, so reasonable that Caro wanted to shake him. Or blacken his other eye. Her hands trembled at the revelation and she could not help but to feel betrayed by her own brother. "I lied to him because you asked it of me."

"Aye. As you should. You're a loyal Sutton."

"I should have been loyal to *him*."

Because I love him.

Jasper took the wine from her hands, which was for the best. She'd been about to either spill it or toss it against the wall. "You did what was right. We all did, in our ways."

If lying to Gavin had kept him safe, she would make the choice again just as she had done. There was no question; she would save his life before any other decision, even if it meant destroying his faith in her.

"He'll never forgive me for this," she whispered, the words torn from her.

"He'll forgive you," Jasper vowed. "Because 'e has to marry you now, the whoreson. No Winter is going to bed my sister without making an honest woman of 'er."

Her brother was serious, she realized. Jasper intended to see her married to Gavin Winter. And while her foolish heart leapt with hope at the thought, the rational part of her mind knew that marrying Gavin without earning his forgiveness would be an even greater blow than watching him turn his back on her this morning. She would not force him to wed her.

And that meant he could never be hers.

* * *

Gavin was bruised and battered, bloody and more miserable than he'd ever been in his life. He could recall all the damned years of his existence now, though the feeling was still strange, all this remembrance after so many weeks of emptiness. Still, he knew the difference.

By the time he reached the back entrance of The Devil's Spawn, the gaming hell he and his half brothers and sister owned and operated together, he felt a bit more like himself. But the homecoming was bittersweet.

Because it didn't feel like home when he rapped on the door and was swept inside the corridor by a guard who looked as if he had just seen a corpse come back to life. It didn't feel like home all the way to his brother Dom's office.

And Gavin knew the reason why. It didn't feel like home because *she* wasn't here.

But everything he'd known with her, he reminded himself, had been a bloody lie.

He could never forgive her for what she had done. She had committed an act of betrayal so deep, so cutting, there would be no healing.

Gavin didn't bother to knock and announce his presence. He threw open the door and crossed the threshold, halting at the sight meeting him.

Within, he found three of his half brothers. Dom, Devil, and Blade. They had been gathered around Dom's desk, and it had appeared as if they were discussing something of great import when he had intruded. Three sets of eyes hit him at once.

Dom, the eldest of them all, responsible for the daily running of The Devil's Spawn, spoke first. "Holy Christ, you look like shit."

He passed a hand over his ravaged face. The bout with Jasper Sutton earlier had not been pretty. "Ain't dead though."

"Thank the Lord for that," Devil said.

Blade cocked his head. "I don't know, brother. You look as if you've recently escaped the body snatchers."

Emotion rose within Gavin, strong and fierce. He had missed his family. He loved them and their antics. Their sallies, their banter, their howls of laughter, their knife-tossing competitions, the way they protected one another no matter what happened.

He was home here, amongst people he could trust.

"I *feel* as if I've escaped the body snatchers," he told Blade wryly. "I've spent the last few weeks at The Sinner's Palace, kept under guard by Jasper Sutton, without an inkling as to who the hell I was."

"You remember us," Dom said. "Your memory has returned?"

"Aye. Why else would I be here?" He searched his brothers' countenances, feeling as if something were amiss.

Dom winced. Devil lowered his gaze. Blade cleared his throat.

His instincts never failed him. Something was wrong. Desperately, terribly wrong.

This was not the bloody welcome he had expected. Unless he was mistaken, there was guilt on every one of their damned faces. Suspicion began to rise.

"Have you nothing to say?" he demanded. "Any of you?"

He'd never known them to hold their tongues. A right vocal lot, the Winter siblings.

"We knew you were with Sutton," Dom said.

What the bloody hell?

He listed on his feet, feeling as if he had taken another blow in addition to the ones Jasper Sutton had landed earlier. Surely his brothers had not known he was being kept at The Sinner's Palace, being fed lies by Jasper and Caro Sutton.

Caro.

His heart gave a pang at the thought of her. She had looked as broken as he had felt this morning, but he had forced himself to walk away. She had deceived him, betrayed him. *Hell*, she had allowed him to ask her to be his wife, to make love to her, and she had never once told him the truth.

There was no excuse for what she had done. She was every bit as heartless and cold as her brother.

"How?" he forced out, his voice hoarse.

Disbelieving.

"Sutton came to Dom," Devil said grimly, stalking forward and catching Gavin in a brotherly hug. "You remember *everything* now?"

"Aye." Gavin extricated himself from Devil's embrace, only to be caught up in a series of awkward hugs. First Dom, then Blade.

"We are happy to have you back among us, brother," Dom said. "Who else knows you are here?"

He thought for a moment. "The guardsman at the door. A few others I passed on my way here. The widow Crawford, who called to me when I descended from the hack which brought me here."

"Sutton sent you here in a hack?" Devil demanded.

"Damn it all to hell," Blade muttered. "This cannot be good. Widow Crawford has the loosest tongue in the East End."

Gavin was more confused than ever. More confused, even, than he had been when he had opened his eyes to find the woman he had naively believed to be his guardian angel hovering over him. He could almost conjure her here and now—her delicate, lavender scent, her full, sensual lips, those wide, hazel eyes and that gleaming auburn hair.

Hell.

Would there ever come a day when he would not want her? When he would not love her? It had been hours, and all he wanted was to race back to her side, to find a way to forget the trespasses she had committed against him.

His overburdened mind, which had been thumping ever since he had arisen that morning to his fully restored memories and which had been pounding mercilessly ever since his bout of fisticuffs with Jasper Sutton, throbbed even more.

"Why did Sutton come to you?" he demanded, trying to make sense of the jagged bits of information he had received thus far.

"He wanted to preserve the truce," Dom said. "I asked him to keep you there until we felt it safe for you to return."

He shook his head. "I don't understand."

"You remember that someone attacked Demon outside Lady Fortune?" Devil asked, frowning. "Do you not?"

"Aye, whoever was after his wine merchant," Gavin said, recalling the day he had visited Demon at Lady Fortune in the wake of the incident.

"We don't think that's the way it happened," Blade told him. "Ambrose Stokes came to Dom after you'd disappeared, claiming someone had been trying to put a price on your head for weeks. He said what happened to Demon had been a mistake. The men hired for the task mistook Demon for you. They killed the wine merchant because he was going to raise a cry, but they didn't finish the job with Demon because after they knocked him on the napper, they got a look at his face and realized he was not you. Davy found him and raised the cry, chasing them off."

"Stokes told me the bastards who attacked Demon came to him asking for aid, but that he declined," Dom added. "They must have acquired more muscle and followed you after you had gotten soused with Demon. They attacked you when you were returning home and then left you for dead outside The Sinner's Palace to try to pin the blame on the Suttons."

Ambrose Stokes was a notorious mercenary known for solving any problem for the right amount of coin. He was a vicious man. Gavin wouldn't trust him as far as he could throw him. Still, he *had* recalled the memory of five men attacking him at once.

"And how much money did Stokes want in return for his information?" Gavin asked, distrustful of the bastard.

"No coin," Dom said. "Stokes is looking to get out of the business. He knows forming an alliance with the Winters will be beneficial to him, and if his information can help us to discover who the hell wants you dead and why, I'll return the favor."

Devil nodded. "We all will."

"But why leave me at The Sinner's Palace?" he demanded, still reeling beneath the weight of all these sudden revelations. "Why not bring me here?"

"Because we wanted whoever is trying to kill you to believe they succeeded," Blade offered, his voice grim. "But now, it's only a matter of time before news that Gavin Winter has risen from the dead is all over the rookeries."

Icy dread slid down his spine, wrapped around his heart. "And who do you think is trying to kill me?"

"Jeremiah Jones," all three of his half brothers said in unison.

CHAPTER 12

After so many weeks of seeing Gavin every day, suddenly spending each day without him had been a more devastating blow than Caro could have anticipated. To keep her mind from thoughts of him, she went to her work room and did what she did best: she returned to her role as the Sutton healer.

Measuring.

Testing.

Studying.

Replenishing her stores.

These were actions which had once given her great pleasure. Now, they did not even provide comfort. Or distraction. Because all she could think about was Gavin.

A knock sounded at her door, and for a moment, her heart leapt, hoping it was him. But the portal opened and Pen appeared.

"I thought I would find you here," her sister said, her countenance wreathed with sympathy.

And a touch of guilt, too, Caro thought. She had discovered that her sister's ailment had been feigned. More of

Jasper's machinations in an effort to keep Caro from spending time with Gavin. She knew he'd been trying to protect her—that Pen and Jasper both had—but that did not mean Caro had entirely forgiven them for their subterfuge. Especially since the nights she had spent singing in the hell had robbed her of precious time with Gavin.

Time she would never be able to regain.

"I am working, Pen," she said on a sigh, not wanting company just now.

Lonely misery was far preferable to a well-intentioned sister attempting to cheer her. There would be no cheering Caro now. She had lost the man she loved. Worse, he was still in danger, and there was nothing she could do to protect or help him because he no longer wanted her in his life.

"As I see and as you usually are." Pen slipped into the work room despite Caro's lack of invitation. "But there is something I thought you should know."

"What can it be, Pen? I'm in a dreadful mood."

"You've been in a dreadful mood since Gavin Winter left," her sister observed, her expression knowing. "You fell in love with him, did you not?"

She closed her eyes and took a deep breath before opening them once more. Thinking about Gavin made her heart hurt. "Yes. I did. But I also spent the last few weeks deceiving him, and I expect he shall never forgive me."

"That is why I thought you should know he is planning to fight Jeremiah Jones," Pen told her. "Aidan knows all about it. It's causing quite a great deal of excitement. Everyone is saying Gavin Winter has risen from the dead."

The pain in her heart turned to ice. "He cannot mean to fight in the state he is in. He is yet healing."

Pen laid a hand on her arm, giving her a soothing pat. "The match is set for three days hence."

Why would he agree to such foolishness? To such dangerous recklessness? Did he not have a care for himself?

"I do not understand why he would agree to the match," she said, struggling to make sense of what her sister had just revealed. "He is in no condition to face an opponent. Indeed, a man in his position should not take such a risk. If he suffers another blow to the head, there is no telling what will happen."

Dear God. She had to stop him. She had to find him and convince him to stop the fight.

But where had he gone?

"The wagers are being placed, and the odds are not in his favor," Pen said softly. "Everyone believes Jeremiah Jones will win and that it will be a fight to the death."

A fight to the death.

She was trembling as violently as a leaf in a wind storm, her stomach lurching. The thought of Gavin fighting an opponent until he breathed his last…it was unthinkable. She could not bear him being injured. Or worse.

"No," she denied, shaking her head. "It cannot be."

"The last man Jeremiah Jones fought died the day after the bout," Pen said. "That is why I have come to you, Caro. Jeremiah Jones is a dangerous man."

Her mind was made. She had to see Gavin. Even if he did not want to speak with her ever again, she needed to try to persuade him against this fight.

"Thank you for telling me, Pen," she told her sister. "I know what I must do."

* * *

Finding Gavin Winter the second time had not proven nearly as easy as finding him the first time had. Caro had gone to The Devil's Spawn but had been denied entry on account of her being female. At the rear entry, she had finally cozened the guard into allowing her inside. Within the maze of halls, she could have wandered forever. In the end, it was Gavin who found her, apparently having been alerted to her presence by the guard.

He came stalking toward her, his handsome face a frozen mask. "What the hell are you doing here?"

She took a moment to drink in the sight of him, so welcome after their days apart, before she shook herself from her thoughts. "I came to see you, Gavin."

He held up his hands, making a sweeping gesture toward himself. "And here I am. Now go."

He did not want to see her. She knew she ought not to be surprised, but she could not deny that his reaction hurt.

"I will not go until you listen to me," she said, holding her ground. "I know you are angry with me for keeping the truth a secret—"

"Angry does not begin to describe it," he interrupted, seething.

Even in his outrage, his posture so rigid and indifferent, his voice cold and cutting, he was beautiful. Beloved. She would never stop loving him. He owned her heart, and he always would.

Whether he wanted it or not.

"I never wished to deceive you," she tried again.

"And yet you did."

She longed to reach for him, to touch him, but she did not dare. The tender lover of several nights before had vanished, and in his place stood a cool, harsh stranger. "Will you not at least hear what I have to say?"

He crossed his arms over his chest. "No."

A dark-haired man peered around one of the doorways behind Gavin. "Chrissakes, Gav, if you're going to have a conversation with your woman, have it in one of the private rooms instead of the damned hall."

Caro's cheeks went hot. She wondered just who the man was and what he had overhead, what he knew of her.

"She ain't my woman," Gavin snarled, glaring at Caro. "She's a Sutton and a liar."

"Whatever she is, I don't want to hear the two of you bickering while I'm balancing the bloody ledgers," the man countered, his voice calm, his tone firm.

"Fine," Gavin growled, moving toward Caro and seizing her arm in a grasp that was not painful but would nevertheless be difficult indeed to extricate herself from. "Come with me, Sutton."

Sutton.

She was no longer Caro to him now.

Pain howled through her as he hauled her into a small salon and closed the door behind them. Not the physical sort of pain but the sort that could crush a woman from the inside out.

He released her instantly, as if he found the very notion of touching her repellent, and with such abruptness, she nearly lost her balance. When he turned his fierce green gaze on her, her tongue refused to cooperate. For a moment, all she could do was think of the man he had been before. Was this angry man before her the true Gavin Winter? Or had she created him with her deception?

"Go on then," he said, "tell me what the devil you are doing here."

"I was told you intend to fight Jeremiah Jones."

His full lips thinned. "Aye, not that it's any concern of yours."

Merciful saints, he intended to do it. What Pen had told her was true. Instinctively, Caro stepped toward him, closing the distance between them, reaching for him. "Gavin, please.

I am begging you not to fight. You are still healing, and from what I have been told, Jeremiah Jones is a ruthless man."

"Save your begging," he snarled, shaking her touch from his arm.

"You will not be able to defend yourself," she continued, fear prodding her despite the rage emanating from him. "I am told he has already killed a man."

"You needn't fret over me, Sutton. I know where your loyalty lies."

She flinched, for the words possessed the force of a blow.

Because they were true. Her loyalty had not been to Gavin as it should have been. Instead, she had kept the truth from him, and she would forever hate herself for the choice she had made. An impossible choice, it was true; either way, she would have hurt someone beloved to her.

"I know you are angry with me," she tried again, "but please do not allow that to cloud your judgment."

"Angry doesn't begin to describe the way I feel," he fumed. "You lied to me. You allowed me to torment myself for weeks, all while you knew who I was. I must have amused you, thinking myself in love with a woman who has no heart."

She deserved his outrage. But despite what he thought of her, she loved him. She loved him more than she had ever imagined possible. And she had lost him, through no one's fault but her own. However, she would be damned if she would allow any harm to befall him because of her actions. She could not bear it if anything would happen to him.

"Regardless of your poor opinion of me, you must know that fighting Jeremiah Jones is akin to going to the gallows. Your injury has made you weak, and you have not regained the strength in your wounded arm."

"The only goddamn thing that made me weak was you," he countered grimly, his voice filled with darkness and bite.

"I'm fighting Jones, and there isn't a bloody thing you can do to stop me."

"If you will not listen to me, then surely you will consult your siblings?" she asked, desperate now. "What have they made of this decision of yours?"

Tears pricked her eyes, ready to be shed. She blinked to hold them back.

"Do not speak of them," he said, his jaw tensed. "They are my blood. You are less than nothing to me."

His words sank into her heart as surely as any blade. She reeled beneath the weight of them, the crushing fear he would forever hate her for what she had done.

"Despise me if you must," she forced herself to say. "But I would far prefer to bear your hatred than for you to be killed in a prizefight. I did not nurse you back to health only to watch you throw yourself to the lions."

His lip curled, but even sneering, he was ruthlessly handsome. "*I'm* the lion, Caro. I may have forgotten for a time, but I remember now. I have you to thank for that. Now get out of my family's hell and out of my life."

Before she could respond, he turned and stalked from the room, leaving her standing there alone. At the slamming of the door at his back, she allowed the tears to fall. She had failed him.

And this time, she feared, there would be no saving him.

* * *

SEEING Caro again had shaken Gavin.

Shaken him so badly that his hands were literally trembling as he stormed to Dom's office. His half brother stood at his entrance, quirking a brow.

"Caro Sutton, I presume?"

Caro.

His Caro.

He had not stopped loving her. Damn it.

Gavin raked his fingers through his hair. "Aye. That is the serpent's name."

"Eh. Didn't look much like a serpent to me."

He gritted his teeth so hard, his jaw ached. "No, she doesn't look like a goddamned serpent. But that does not mean she ain't one."

"You've been angry ever since you returned," Dom said.

"And why wouldn't I be? I nearly cocked up my toes, spent weeks without recalling a single damned piece of my life, my own family left me to rot at a Sutton gaming hell, and I've been kept a prisoner and lied to all because the lot of you thought I would be safer hiding like a damned lad behind his mother's skirts."

As he finished the diatribe, he became aware his voice had risen to a roar. But it felt good to unleash some more of his fury, damn it. Dom was not wrong. He had been bloody furious since his return. They had all—every last one of them, from his family to Jasper Sutton to Caro—robbed him of his right to choose what was best for him.

Dom winced. "I know you do not see it as we did, but we made the decision we felt was best for you."

"I should have been the one to make that choice."

His half brother shook his head. "As you are now, agreeing to fight the man we believe was responsible for trying to see you killed and for nearly having Demon murdered as well?"

"A strange thing happens to a man when he has nothing left to lose," Gavin said, meaning those words with everything in him. "He forgets what fear is, because it doesn't matter any longer."

"Gav, you have much to lose," Dom countered, frowning

in that way of his that suggested he was the wiser older brother, the leader of the family, and he knew better.

But not in this instance, he bloody well didn't.

"No. I do not. I already lost everything I wanted."

And that everything had been Caro. How dare she lie to him as she had, then come rushing here to beg him not to fight Jeremiah Jones? As if she cared. *Ha!* If she had truly loved him as she had claimed, she would have told him the truth when she'd had the chance. Not when it had been too late, when he had caught her in a lie.

"You are speaking of Caro Sutton, are you not?" Dom asked gently.

"I am speaking of the life I had before," he said, though that was not entirely true. "I was the best prizefighter in England, damn it, and now I'll never regain the strength I had."

Admitting as much to Dom was far easier. His pride was too strong to allow Caro to know he believed she was right, that fighting Jeremiah Jones was a damned stupid thing to do. Jones was taller, with a more muscular body than Gavin had possessed even before he'd spent weeks first as an invalid and later chasing after Caro Sutton's skirts.

In the wake of his return to the bosom of the family he loved, Gavin had made a realization. If Jeremiah Jones had indeed paid to have him murdered to avoid their match and be named the best prizefighter in England by eliminating Gavin as his competition, that meant the man would only try again. And that also meant the stupid bastard could hire more dimwitted criminals who attacked the wrong men instead of him.

He would not put his family in danger. Instead, he would face the problem. Let Jeremiah Bloody Bastard Jones meet him in a match he knew he would win. As he'd said to Dom,

Gavin had nothing left to lose. What was one more bout, for the safety of his family?

"Sodding hell, Gav." Dom's oath shook Gavin from his troubled thoughts. "If you know you don't have the strength you had before, then why the devil have you goaded Jones into accepting this fight?"

He met his brother's gaze, unwavering. "Because Gavin Winter rose from the grave, and I'm either going to put Jones in his, or die trying. Either way, my family will be free. I'll not have another of you harmed because of me."

"I do not like it, Gav." Dom's expression was hard. Concerned. "Not one damned bit. It's dangerous, and Jones was doing everything in his power—including hiring assassins—the last bloody time you were going to fight him."

"You don't have proof it was Jones who wanted me dead, and you don't have to like my choices, Dom. I'm doing what I must. You made decisions on my behalf when I was weak and wounded, but now, it's my turn. I'll face Jones, and that is final."

CHAPTER 13

Caro had decided that if she wanted to keep Gavin from putting his life in danger, she would have to take action. To that end, she found one Mr. Jeremiah Jones at a tavern in the rookeries, surrounded by dangerous-looking men, a tankard of ale in his meaty paw of a fist. Drury Lane vestals—women in various states of undress, some with their breasts on display like the wares on an apple cart—were strewn about. The floor was sticky with years of spilled drinks and blood, and the room was rife with tobacco smoke, raucous laughter, and curious stares.

The moment she had crossed the threshold, entering the dank, forbidding den of thieves, the air seemed to freeze. She was uncomfortably aware of all the curious eyes upon her, for she was a new face in what would be a sea of the familiar, especially the women who frequented the Beggar's Purse. Thank heavens Randall was awaiting her in the carriage on the street; if he had not accompanied her, she would have feared what would become of her in such an establishment.

Her discreet inquiries, coupled with the passing of coin,

had led her to a mountainous man with a buxom blonde in his lap, his hand down her bodice, another up her skirts.

"Is that him?" she asked the man who had volunteered the information she sought in exchange for two guineas.

"Aye." The man nodded. "That is 'imself."

"Excellent." Though the sight of the man she would need to confront hardly felt excellent in that moment, she knew it was what she must do. She swept across the disgusting floor, skirting tables and debauchery in varying degrees, until she reached Jeremiah Jones.

Randall awaited her, she reminded herself as her courage faltered, and he would protect her with his very life, though she hoped this night would not come to that. Still, they were in a particularly ugly, mangy part of the rookeries. One never knew what was going to happen.

"Jeremiah Jones?" she asked.

He cocked his head, eying Caro rudely as he squeezed the bare breast of the woman on his lap, making her giggle. "Who wants to know?"

The woman's giggle sounded forced, and Caro tried to thrust that, and the blatant nudity, from her mind.

"Caroline Sutton," she said, lifting her chin. "Jasper Sutton's sister."

Jones raised a pale brow. "I know 'im. Can't say as I like 'im much."

Caro remained undeterred. "I'm sure the feeling is mutual, sir. But I didn't come here to speak with you about my brother."

"Oh? And aren't you a bold one? Did you come looking for me this evening, love?" He leered at her even as he plucked at the nipple of the unfortunate woman in his lap.

The blonde's head lolled back, and Caro wondered if the woman was hopelessly soused, or if she had merely numbed herself to her surroundings. Likely, a combination of both.

"I did," Caro confirmed. "I need to speak with you."

"Speak?" The giant's hand moved rudely beneath the blonde's gown. "Is that what you're callin' it?"

The men at his table guffawed. The woman on his lap squirmed, then let out a moan that sounded quite rehearsed.

"That is what I'm calling it because that is what it *is*, Mr. Jones," she said coldly, reminding herself that confronting this despicable man was what she needed to do to help Gavin.

And to keep him from becoming Jeremiah Jones's next victim.

Jones grinned, revealing a chipped tooth she had no doubt had been damaged in one of his bareknuckle matches. "We can talk all you like. The three of us." He squeezed the breast of the woman on his lap once more. "Isn't that right, pet?" he growled into the woman's ear.

The woman ogled Caro. "She's a small one. Tiny bubbies, Jerry. Wot do y'want with 'er? I'll make you 'appy, I will. No need for 'er."

Caro tried not to grimace at the suggestion she join Jones and the woman in his lap in something carnal in nature. "My business is with you, Mr. Jones. No one else. Is there a private room we can visit so we may better converse?"

"What's in it for me?" he asked, swilling his ale.

"Balsam," she told him, hoping the money she could promise him—every last ha'penny she possessed for her part in running The Sinner's Palace—would be enough to persuade Jones to cry off the match with Gavin.

"Jasper Sutton's sister offering me coin. I'm curious, I am." Jones winked, then unceremoniously shoved the blonde woman from his lap, delivering a sound slap to her rump as he did so. "I'll be back, Mary. Wait for me."

The woman tugged at her bodice, barely gaining her footing before being hauled into the lap of one of the other men about the table. "The name's Margaret, lovey," she called toward Jones.

But the great, hulking beast had already risen from his seat. And he was looming over Caro now with a predatory smile curving his lips. "Come with me, sweeting. I'll 'ear what you 'ave to say."

She swallowed down a lump of fear, telling herself that she was a Sutton. She had come of age in the rookeries. There was nothing she had not seen, done, or heard. And yet, she could not shake the inexplicable sense of dread filling her, curling its icy fingers around her heart.

There was something about Jeremiah Jones... The man radiated evil.

Still, if it meant keeping Gavin safe, she would face any demon, fight any battle.

Because she loved him, and because she owed him that much and more.

She followed Jeremiah Jones through the boisterous rabble in the Beggar's Purse, to a private room.

* * *

Gavin had an aching back and head, a mouth that tasted of sour arrack, and a dim recollection of what had happened the night before, beyond all the spirits he'd swilled with his brothers Demon, Blade, and Devil. Strange how consuming too much of the poison could decimate his memory, same as the beating he'd taken to the idea pot.

He groaned as his eyes fluttered open, taking in his surroundings. It appeared to be a drawing room. Quite fine, too. Gilt and polish everywhere, oil paintings hanging on the walls, a vase of fresh-cut flowers on a gleaming table for Chrissakes. But it wasn't the room that troubled him so much as it was the sight of his arms and legs lashed to a gilt chair.

God's blood, he couldn't move.

On a roar, Gavin thrashed, attempting to free himself. But the knots held tight.

Frantically, he sifted through his mind for memories of the night before.

After his interviews with Caro and Dom, Gavin had thrown himself into the one solace he'd always had before he'd been attacked—physical exertion. He had challenged one of the guards to a match and had found himself rusty but not as weak as he had supposed he would be. The moment fists were moving, that part of himself returned, even if the strength of his wounded arm had yet to be regained.

Even if it would never be regained, he was still Gavin Winter, *curse it*, and he was a damned fine fighter. Following the pitched battle with the guard, Demon, Blade, and Devil had found him. Indeed, all had been well until his brothers had swooped in and plied him with drink. He should have known the three of them were not to be trusted.

He recalled Blade pouring more arrack into his glass, and he recalled precious little after that.

Suddenly, the door to the drawing room opened, and an elegant blonde crossed the threshold with haste, closing the door at her back.

Understanding dawned.

He had been spirited away by his own bloody sister.

"Gen," he growled, struggling furiously at the bonds holding him to the chair. "What the hell are you doing?"

"Protecting you, brother, just as you once protected me," she said simply. "I won't be responsible for you cocking up your toes. Bad enough it almost happened once."

Damn her. He should have known. Gen was fearless, stubborn, and did whatever she pleased, including marrying a marquess and starting the first gaming hell of its kind, for ladies only. She was also protective to her marrow.

"I don't need your protection, and you're a fine lady now. Kidnapping gents in the East End ought to be the business of murderers and thieves."

"In this instance, it's the business of a sister who loves her brother and is determined to see that he does not do something incredibly foolish, like fight a beast of a man when you haven't yet regained the strength in your wounded arm."

Her voice was calm. As if she had not seen him tied to a chair.

He rocked on the chair, and the thing tipped from side to side. "Untie me and let me go, Gen."

"No."

"Damn it, Gen," he growled, furiously tugging at his bonds and making the chair dance a frantic jig. "This is madness."

But his sister remained unmoved. "If you keep carrying on, you'll upend the chair and hurt yourself, Gav. I'd settle myself if I were you."

"How long do you intend to keep me here?" he demanded, fearing he already knew the answer.

"Until you get some sense in your napper or until the appointed time for the fight passes, or until we can see Jeremiah Jones gets the punishment he deserves, whichever comes first."

"I need to piss. This mad scheme of yours won't work."

That much was true. Had his sister never risen to the regret of a night ill-spent? Mouth that tasted as if he'd been licking an attic stair and an urgent desire to find a chamber pot. Sometimes for more than one reason.

His sister grimaced. He could tell she had not thought that far.

"I'll not be helping you with *that*," she said, "but I suppose one of the footmen might."

Good Christ. Gen was a Bedlamite.

"Bloody hell, Gen. You've brought me to your townhome? What the devil were you thinking?" he asked, for he knew quite well all the efforts she had undertaken to make herself more suitable in the eyes of society and her husband's judgmental aristocratic family. Her father-in-law the duke would be livid should word of this become fodder for gossip.

She blinked. "I was thinking that my brother is being a complete arsehole, and he needs rescuing from himself. That's what I was thinking. Jeremiah Jones tried to have you killed, and he almost had Demon murdered instead. Now you've gone about announcing you are back from the dead and ready to face Jones in your fight, undoing all the good work our family has done in keeping you a secret."

His siblings all thought they knew better than he. Had it never occurred to any of them that he knew what he was doing? That he understood and accepted the risks he was taking? That they were *necessary*?

"Your husband can't know you've done this."

"Max? Of course he does." She smiled. "Abducting you was his idea, in fact. Well, his and Dom's. The two of them happened upon the notion simultaneously, and it is the only way to keep you from doing anything else that is reckless or stupid."

Gavin rolled his eyes heavenward. "Lord, I'm begging you. Have I not been punished enough in this life? Did you need to surround me with madmen and madwomen, too?"

She kicked him in the shins with her slipper-shod foot, a gesture that was at odds with the genteel ladylike vision she presented—a pale-ivory muslin gown to her favored breeches, her hair styled in elegant perfection, jewels at her throat.

"Whilst you've got the Lord's ear, mayhap you should ask him why you're being such an idiot," Gen told him.

"*I'm* being an idiot? You're the one who had your own brother get soused and then had him tied to a goddamn drawing room chair."

Her brows rose. "Oh, Gav. I'd not be using the Lord's name in vain if I were you. You were just having a dialogue with him. And who says I'm the one who had you get soused? I did not join you and our other brothers last night."

"But if you know of it, and if I woke to find myself tied to one of your damned drawing room chairs, then you are indeed a part of this nonsensical plan."

When he managed to find his way out of this bloody drawing room, he was going to box his sister's ears. Or insist she name her firstborn son after him. Now that he thought upon it, the latter held some merit. Fancy that, a future duke named after an East End bastard prizefighter.

"How is keeping you from getting yourself killed a nonsensical plan?" she asked calmly.

"You should trust me to take action on my own instead of abducting me and hiding me in a drawing room. From the moment I returned to the bloody family flock and learned the truth of what had happened, I have been thinking of nothing other than what I can do to end this before anyone else is hurt."

That was not entirely true. He had also been thinking of Caro.

Endlessly.

But he was not about to admit that to his sister now.

Gen frowned at him. "Your solution is to dangle yourself as a lure to that murderous bastard?"

"If Jones wants me dead, let him have a chance at it," he said calmly. "Far better me than anyone else."

"No." Gen shook her head vehemently. "We are not allowing you to put yourself in danger again."

"Who the devil is *we*?" he demanded.

"Your family who loves you," was her stubborn reply.

"Gen, you've got to let me go," he said, trying for reason.

"No, I do not. We have all decided this is the best course. You will remain here until you are no longer a threat to yourself."

"Tied to a bleeding chair?" he shouted. "Genevieve Winter, I demand you cease this nonsense!"

"I am no longer Genevieve Winter," she reminded him calmly, "and I am not going to listen to you, either. We almost lost you once, Gav, and we're not about to lose you again."

With that pronouncement, Gen turned on her heel and began making her exit, enough airs on display to rival a queen. She stopped at the threshold, glancing back at him. "I'll send a footman along soon."

Damn it to hell.

"I'm not going to piss in a chamber pot with the help of one of your servants, Gen."

She ignored him and slipped from the room.

"Gen!" he hollered after her. "Gen, curse your hide, come back here!"

But his cries went unheeded.

If he wanted to get himself out of this latest scrape, he was going to have to bloody well take action.

* * *

Gavin had been tied to the damned chair for what seemed like an eternity.

He had struggled against his binding, but that had only served to make the knots tighter. A footman had come to aid him in relieving himself and he had chased the man away. He would wait until his damned teeth were floating in his head, and he vowed it.

His siblings had apparently decided once more that they knew what was best for him. While he could not deny the plan he had set into motion regarding Jeremiah Jones was treacherous, it was the only way he could protect his family and liberate himself from the cloud of impending doom which seemed to be looming over his head. They had to understand that there was no way any of them would be safe until he and Jeremiah Jones had their reckoning.

Suddenly, the drawing room door opened, jolting Gavin from his thoughts. He could not have been more shocked if the devil himself had crossed the threshold.

And indeed, mayhap he had.

Jasper Sutton strode into the room, wearing his perpetual scowl. Gen was at his heels, her husband Sundenbury at her side. Neither of them appeared impressed by their guest. Gavin could not blame them—despite Sutton's keeping him a secret to prolong the truce with his family, being lied to and imprisoned for weeks had not left him inclined to like the villain.

"Sutton," Gavin greeted, unable to keep from needling him. "If they've sent you here to help me take a piss while I'm tied to the chair, I'm afraid I'll have to decline."

He was being crude in front of his sister and his brother-in-law, but damn it, Gavin was in desperate circumstances at the moment. As evidenced by his current position.

"The only thing I'll be helping you with is getting into a grave if something happens to my sister because of your sorry arse," Sutton growled.

His gut clenched, fear spiking through him. "Caro?"

"Aye." Sutton sneered. "Though you ain't fit to speak her name."

"Mr. Sutton," Sundenbury said, sounding very much like the aristocrat he was, "I'll thank you to keep your tone civil before my wife and brother-in-law."

"The brother-in-law you've lashed to the chair?" Sutton eyed the marquess, his brows raised. "Don't act the fucking angels with me, the two of you."

"I may be a marchioness, but that does not mean I can't plant you a facer," Gen cautioned.

Gavin had no doubt she would do it, too. *He* had taught her how to punch.

But none of this squabbling was getting to the heart of the matter, and Gavin's own heart felt as if it were being squeezed by a merciless, invisible fist. "Stubble it, the lot of you. Sutton, what is happening with Caro? Is she in danger?"

Sutton's expression was rigid, but there was a hint of fear hiding beneath his composure, and that was what made Gavin's inner worry heighten to a frenzy. "Of course she's in danger, you coxcomb. She's been taken by Jeremiah Jones."

His gut curdled. "What do you mean she's been taken?"

"She went looking for the bastard last night," Sutton elaborated. "Apparently, she was trying to pay him not to face you in the match. She took one of my guards with her but entered the Beggar's Purse alone, and that bastard seized her and left through the rear. By the time my man went checking on her, the pair were long gone. I received a note from Jones this morning, telling me I need to give him one hundred guineas or Mr. Gavin Winter himself if I want to get Caro back. Since you're the reason she's been spirited away by that—"

"Yes," Gavin interrupted, not wanting to waste another moment on useless speech. "I'll go with you. Gen, untie me."

"Gav," she said softly, her face contorted with worry, "you can't face Jones alone."

"He won't be alone. I'll be with him," Sutton said, nodding

at him in what Gavin suspected was the closest show of approval the man would offer.

"There is no time to waste," Gavin urged. "Caro could be in terrible danger, and she needs us."

And right then and there, it hit him with stunning, unalterable clarity: he needed her, too. God, how he needed her. In the face of losing her, all his anger and outrage fell away. He needed to be where she was, to face Jeremiah Jones, to end this battle, and to make Caro his, just as she had been meant to be all along.

Gen sighed. "Are you certain this is what you must do, Gav?"

He met his sister's gaze, unflinching. "I love her, Gen. I'd do anything to protect her."

"Fine way you have of showing it," Sutton snarled.

And Gavin could not blame him. When Caro had come to him the day before, if he had not been so bloody set upon clinging to his anger, if he had just forgiven her, she would not have gone looking for Jones. She had done so in an effort to protect him. Because she loved him.

And now, he was going to fight for her, damn it.

"Cut the ropes, Gen," he said.

She nodded, her eyes glistening. "Come back to me, brother."

"I'll do my best," he promised as Sundenbury set about cutting his bindings.

In truth, all he cared about was saving Caro.

To the devil with himself.

CHAPTER 14

Going to Jeremiah Jones had proven a dreadful, terrible mistake. Caro acknowledged it to herself as she stood, bound and miserable, in the corner of the shabby rooms where he had taken her the night before. Their meeting in the private rooms of the Beggar's Purse had quickly proven disastrous, and largely because she had forgotten the cardinal Sutton rule.

She had been unarmed. The endless span of hours she'd been forced to spend alone, wondering what would befall her, had turned into an equally endless round of self-chastisement. One which continued now, as the morning waned into afternoon and she remained tied and alone, cold, tired, and hungry.

Stupid, stupid Caro. You reckless, witless fool.

She'd gone in search of Jeremiah Jones without preparation and without proper thought, so desperate had she been to keep Gavin from fighting the man. She'd had no knife, no pistol hidden in her reticule, nothing but Randall awaiting her outside. And even that attempt at protecting herself had proven fruitless when Jones had extracted a small, lethal-looking pistol from his coat and ordered her to leave the tavern through a rear entrance.

She'd had no other choice, she reminded herself.

But that did not mean she had not spent the sleepless night berating herself for what she had done. She had gone to Jeremiah Jones thinking the money she had to offer would have been sufficient lure to keep him from facing Gavin in the match. But a swift change had overtaken him during her explanation. Sensing the danger in the air, she'd begun creeping steadily toward the door. That had been when Jones had withdrawn his pistol and told her he had a different idea in mind for her.

You just may be useful to me, Miss Caroline Sutton, he'd said, before telling her he wouldn't hesitate to shoot her if she cried out for help or tried to run. He'd forced her into a hack, and she'd spent their trip to his dingy rooms frantically plotting a means of escape. But Jones had been a step ahead. He'd made certain to threaten the hackney driver and a young child and his mother they passed on the street. Rather than take the risk he would attempt to hurt another or her, Caro had gone.

When they were within his rooms, she had frantically seized upon a pitcher, attempting to strike him with it. But Jones had been faster. He'd knocked the pitcher from her hand, sending it to the floor where it smashed into hundreds of jagged porcelain shards. And then he had slapped her with biting force.

The blow had been enough to make dark stars speckle her vision and to stun her sufficiently that he'd had her wrists bound with a soiled neckcloth before she could so much as fight him off. She'd been no match for Jones' intimidating size and beast-like strength.

But the mystery of what he intended to do with her, and why, remained. It had been looming in all the hours since his disappearance. The more time that passed, the more heightened her worry became. She had been pacing the chamber for what must have been hours as daylight grew increasingly brighter through the lone window. Her search of the room had yielded nothing thus far that would enable her to cut herself free of the binding.

But surely, surely, there must be something, somewhere. A weapon. Something sharp…

That was when she noticed it, a jagged shard of white porcelain peeking from beneath the bed. Jones had swept up the broken pitcher before leaving, but apparently, he had missed a piece.

With a cry of sheer relief, she fell to her knees on the stained carpets and seized the broken piece of crockery. Holding it carefully between her wrists, she began sawing at the neckcloth. Her fingers, cramping from the tightness of her bonds, made her drop the shard to the floor. Taking a deep, calming breath, she picked it back up and began again.

Her heart was pounding, her hands trembling. In the hall beyond the door, she heard voices and footsteps and she tried to work faster, praying it was not him, and that she would have enough time to free herself and escape before Jones returned.

But just as she was beginning to make progress, her tormentor appeared on the threshold, a pistol once more pointed directly at her heart. The shard of porcelain fell from her fingers in defeat. She did her best to hide it with her gown, to feign nonchalance so that he would not notice she had been trying to escape her binding.

"Time to come with me, Caroline Sutton," he drawled. "I'm taking you to your brother, and after that I'll be taking Gavin Winter to Rothisbone."

Cold, hard dread filled her stomach.

* * *

Gavin was doing his damnedest to remain calm, but it certainly wasn't easy. He was out of his mind with worry for Caro, and he was scared as hell that Jones had harmed her or worse. If he had, nothing and no one would stop Gavin from beating the bastard to death.

"Calm yourself, Winter," Jasper Sutton told him. "You're going to wear a goddamn hole in my carpets and I've just had them replaced."

He stalked the length of Sutton's office and pinned Caro's brother with a glare. Sutton had arranged for the meeting with Jeremiah Jones to occur at The Sinner's Palace. Neutral territory. In true Winter fashion, Gavin's siblings had not been content to keep their beaks out of the situation.

They'd initially demanded Jones come to The Devil's Spawn until Sutton had correctly pointed out such a meeting place would only serve to make Jones suspicious. As it was, Sutton had replied to Jones' note confirming he now had Gavin Winter in his custody at The Sinner's Palace and he was ready to make a trade. If their plan of battle was to work, they needed Jones to believe Sutton was willing to surrender Gavin in exchange for Caro's safe return.

"How am I to be calm when that rotter has Caro?" he snarled, though he knew Sutton was not wrong in this, the jibe about the carpets aside.

Demon was at his side, planting a calming hand on his shoulder. "Try to remain calm, brother. I know this is deuced difficult, but you've got to stay strong."

"Trying," he bit out.

Trying and failing.

Caro was out there somewhere, in the clutches of a brutal beast, and he was the reason. What if Jones had hurt her? What if she was in pain? What if she was afraid?

He would never be able to forgive himself for clinging to his pride and his anger instead of to his love for her. When this bloody business was over, he was going to tell her. He hoped to God he would have the chance.

"Try 'arder," Sutton snapped at him, shaking him from his apprehensions.

Whenever the man started speaking like he'd been born in the rookeries, Jasper Sutton was worried. And for all that Gavin still resented Sutton for keeping him at The Sinner's Palace under a pretense, he knew Sutton loved Caro.

Gavin loved her, too.

He supposed that did not mean Sutton was all bad.

"Think about the plan instead," Dom urged Gavin, his tone calmer, kinder.

Gen and the legitimate Winters were the only siblings missing from this particular meeting. Gen was carrying a child and none of them—Sundenbury included—would countenance her joining them for a meeting with a madman. And this wasn't the fight of the legitimate Winters, though Gavin had no doubt Devereaux would have gladly joined them had they sent word to him.

There were enough Winters lining the halls of The Sinner's Palace as it was.

"The plan," Gavin repeated slowly, forcing his spinning mind to settle upon it, for their actions were important. What they did could be the difference between life and death, between Caro's safety and…

Nay. Do not think about that now, Gav. Think about saving her. Think about how much you need her. Think about what you must do.

A rap sounded on the door, and then was followed by three knocks in quick succession. Everyone in the room was suddenly, instantly on edge.

Sutton stood. "Jones is here. Winters, hide yourselves."

With the push of a mechanism on the wall behind Sutton's desk, the shelving popped open, allowing for a hidden chamber. Gavin could only guess at what purpose such a room ordinarily served. In this instance, it was to be where his brothers would wait while Gavin and Sutton faced Jeremiah Jones. There was a mechanism within the room by which those inside could open the panel should the need arise.

"No emerging unless I say so," Sutton warned.

Dom, Devil, Blade, and Demon reluctantly shuffled into the room. There was a brace of candles lit within, but the space was incredibly cramped for four large Winter men.

"Do not betray our trust, Sutton," Devil warned, an icy edge to his voice just before the door closed.

Trust and *Sutton*? Once, those two words would never have been married in a sentence. But now...well, Gavin *did* trust the man. If he wanted to save Caro, who was also a Sutton, he had to.

"Are you ready, Winter?" Sutton asked, taking up his position behind his desk.

"Ready," Gavin said, feeling for the tiny pistol hidden in his coat.

Another knock sounded. Just one.

"Come," Sutton called.

Everything within Gavin tensed and tightened as the door opened.

Caro stood on the threshold, a pistol pressed to her ribs, hands bound by a bit of dirty cloth, and a bruise on her cheek. Gavin's heart lurched. At her side was Jeremiah Jones. The bastard was grinning as if he had just been declared the champion. The two of them crossed the threshold as one. Sutton nodded for the guard to close the door to the office.

Holding himself in place required all the restraint Gavin possessed. He wanted to run to Caro, to haul her away from

Jones, but he didn't dare move. Not with the pistol in her side.

"Gavin Winter," Jones said. "We meet again."

"Jones," he spat. "Let her go. Your quarrel is with me."

"You promised to exchange my sister," Sutton added, his voice hard. "Release her now."

"He means to kill you, Gavin!" Caro blurted, her voice choked with fear.

"Shut your gob, or I'll shoot you," Jones threatened, tightening his hold on her.

"I won't." Caro shook her head, tears streaming down her cheeks. "I won't let him hurt you again, Gavin. He's the one responsible for the attack on you, for the attack on your brother."

"Here now," Sutton said calmly. "That's enough out of you, sister. Who gives a goddamn if Jones aims to murder Winter? One less bastard in the world."

Caro gasped, turning her gaze on her brother. "Jasper, how could you say that?"

"Easy," Sutton claimed. "I'm a Sutton, ain't I? My loyalty is to you."

Gavin forced himself to recall the plan, just as Dom had urged him. "You lied to me, you whoreson," he said to Sutton. "You told me I'd not come to harm beneath your roof."

Sutton shrugged, his countenance devoid of emotion. "I lied."

"Time to face me," Jones taunted Gavin. "A final match."

A shiver passed down Gavin's spine, for he knew Jones had no intention of fighting him fairly. He meant to see him dead, one way or another.

Sutton withdrew a pistol, pointing it at Gavin's heart. "You'll go with Jones now, and I'll have my sister back, and whatever the hell he does with your arse is your problem, Winter."

"No!" Caro cried out. "Gavin, you cannot go with him. I beg you."

"I ain't stupid, Sutton," Jones said. "Place your bleeding pistol on the desk, and then I'll release the girl."

"More than 'appy to, my fine fellow," Sutton said, making a grand show of lowering his weapon and sliding it to the very edge of his intricately carved desk, well beyond his reach. As he did so, he knocked on the surface of the desk, just beside the weapon.

It was a curious gesture, but Gavin was too caught up in watching Caro to give a damn. As long as Jones released her safely, he would take his chances with the bastard. He had a pistol hidden in his coat. The moment they were no longer in danger of Caro or anyone else being harmed, he would try to defend himself.

Unease swept over Gavin, and he sent up a silent, desperate prayer as he watched Jones lower the pistol and give Caro a shove toward Sutton. Caro moved in the direction of her brother, and then suddenly stumbled, falling to the floor.

Scarcely a moment passed between Caro's fall and the gunshot which followed. Terror clawed at Gavin, and for a moment, he believed Caro had been wounded. His mind was scarcely able to comprehend what had happened. A panel of Sutton's desk had blown apart, splintered wood littering the carpet. Crimson was spreading on a dazed Jones' shirt, his chest covered in gore. The gun he'd been pointing at Caro had fallen to the floor. Gasping, and making the most wretched of sounds, Jones collapsed. Caro's head had popped up.

Relief washed over him as understanding gradually hit. Somehow, Sutton had fired a weapon which had been secreted within his desk, because the pistol he had willingly capitulated remained on the surface, untouched. But the particulars didn't signify to him at the moment. All that did was one woman.

Caro's hazel gaze met his and held. "Gavin!" she cried.

"Caro." He started for her, not giving a damn about anyone or anything else.

She was all he saw, all he wanted.

He fell to the carpet at her knees, splinters of wood piercing his flesh. Still, he did not care. Dimly, he was aware of the roars of his brothers as they rushed from their hiding place, of Sutton ordering someone to haul Jones from the room. He wrapped Caro in his arms, burying his face in her hair. "Are you hurt, my angel, my love?"

"No," she said.

A flurry of movement and activity surrounded them. Gavin discounted it all, because she was safe. She was safe, and she was in his arms, and she was the most beautiful, beloved sight he had ever seen.

He kissed her. There was no elegance in the act, no seduction or persuasion. Rather, it was a hard, desperate mashing of his mouth upon hers. It was the measure of his relief, his love, his gratitude that she had not been harmed, that she was alive and so was he. Their teeth clacked together. They were both weeping, and the salt of their tears was on their cheeks, pouring down their faces, slipping into their kiss.

Relief and love mingled, the emotions so profound, he scarcely knew what to do with them, what to say. He felt as he had when he had first awoken after being so near to death. Only this time, it was far different than the last. Because this time, he knew who he was, and he knew who she was. And this time, he understood how damned rare it was to have a love like theirs and how close he had come to losing it, first because of his own pride and then because of the machinations of a madman.

He was not going to squander this second chance.

He was going to cling to it—and Caro—with both hands.

He raised his head at last and gazed down at her, hating the bruise that marred her cheek for the pain it had caused her. Hated knowing he was responsible for everything that had befallen her.

"I thought I had lost you," he said, the words torn from him.

"I thought you were going to go with Jones," she returned, tears still sliding down. "He was so intent upon becoming the champion, he would have done anything, Gavin. He would have murdered you."

"He did not have the chance for that," he told her. "Thanks to your brother."

He glanced around them to find Sutton stalking in their direction, a grim expression on his face. "Get up, the two of you. I ain't kneeling in the splinters."

Gavin rose and helped Caro to stand as well, belatedly realizing her wrists were still bound. "Christ. Does anyone have a knife?"

Blade stepped forward, revealing a gleaming, sharp-edged dagger. "Happy to aid my future sister-in-law. Assuming you'll accept his rotten hide, of course."

Caro flushed prettily, her gaze going to Gavin as she held her arms outstretched for Blade to slice through the linen binding her. "He has to wish to marry me before I can accept."

He swallowed against a rush of emotion. "I do. I want to marry you, Caro, if you will have me."

"Damned right you are going to marry her, Winter," Sutton said, skewering him with a pointed glare. "You'll make an honest woman of her, or you'll find yourself no better than Jones."

He was not entirely certain Sutton was engaging in

hyperbole, and he did deserve a sound thrashing for having bedded Caro before marrying her. He could admit as much.

"You do not need to threaten me, Sutton," he said. "I love your sister."

"Deuced strange conversation to be having with your future wife's brother," Sutton sneered. "Tell her you love her. She's the one who needs to hear it."

Duly chastised, Gavin turned back to Caro, whose hands were now free. He took them in his, raising them to his lips for frantic, fervent kisses. "I love you, Caro. My heart has always been waiting to find yours. I knew it before, and I know it now. When I discovered you had been keeping who I was a secret from me, I was angry, and I clung to that anger and my pride instead of to our love. I almost got you killed because of it."

"No." She shook her head, clasping his face in her hands. There were calluses on her fingers, and he loved them, loved her strength, her intelligence, her innate goodness. "I should never have lied to you. It was wrong. I wanted to make amends for my mistakes, and that is why I went to Jones. I thought I could pay him to keep from facing you in the match."

"I loved that desk, you know," Sutton said, reminding Gavin he was still standing about, along with his own brothers.

"How did you do it?" Dom asked, sounding fascinated as he took in the splintered desk.

Sutton grinned. "I kept a pistol hidden within, mounted and loaded. Through a mechanism I designed with the help of my gunsmith, all I need to do is pull a lever within the desk, and it pulls the trigger."

"I'll be needing to speak with your gunsmith," Dom replied thoughtfully.

Sutton grinned. "For the right price."

"Come along then, all of you," Demon said, gesturing toward Gavin and Caro. "We should give the two of them some privacy."

"Stokes is going to see to Jones?" Devil asked Sutton, ever the practical one amongst them.

"Aye," Sutton said. "Stokes will handle everything."

Blade nodded. "Good. Although, I think you're going to have to see the carpet replaced again, Sutton."

"Blood is surprisingly easy to remove from dark carpets," Sutton said as the men left the room, their voices trailing behind them. "Why the hell do you think I chose this pattern?"

When the door had at last closed and they were alone in Jasper Sutton's office, the smell of gun smoke acrid in the air but the swelling tide of hope and love rising around them, Gavin dipped his head toward Caro. "Will you marry me, Caro Sutton? Will you be my wife and join these two mad families of ours in the greatest truce of all?"

Her arms went around his neck. "I will."

"I love you, Caro," he said again. He had spoken the words to her before, but this was different. They were alone. He wanted there to be no doubt between them.

"Oh, Gavin. I love you, too." She sniffled. "I thought I had lost you, and I would not have blamed you if you had never forgiven me for keeping the truth from you. My loyalty to you should have been stronger."

"You've more than proven your loyalty to me," he said, humbled by what she had done, all to save him. "You found me that day, and you could have left me. But instead, you saved me. You saved me, and I fell in love with you as I saw what a caring, kind, intelligent woman you are. A gifted healer, devoted to helping others. And then, even after I had turned my back on you, you still tried to save me, putting yourself in grave danger."

"I would do it again." Her lower lip trembled, calling to be kissed. "I would do everything again just for the chance to be with you, Gavin Winter. Just for the chance to love you and to be your wife."

He brushed his mouth over hers once, twice. Her lips were smooth and warm, an invitation he could not resist. It was like coming home. "My God, Caro Sutton. What did I ever do to deserve you?"

"You incited the wrath of a Bedlamite and nearly got yourself killed on no less than two occasions," she pointed out, sounding like Sutton.

He grinned, drunk on relief and love and *her*. "From this moment forward, I swear that the only Bedlamite whose wrath I shall incite will be your brother's. I can only hope Sutton won't attempt to kill me."

"He would never," Caro said, smiling back at him. "Believe it or not, Jasper has a good heart."

Gavin would have laughed at that—more proof that Caro was an angel among mere mortals—but he had to admit that Jasper Sutton wasn't as much of a ruthless arse as he had once supposed him to be.

"I don't think he likes me much," he said mildly, because he had his arms full of Caro, and that was an excellent armful indeed. All his cares had seemed to fade away, his mind suddenly making sense of the wild moments before Sutton had fired his hidden weapon earlier. "You pretended to fall when Jones released you. You knew your brother was going to fire the hidden pistol, did you not?"

She nodded. "We all know about the secret pistol in his desk. The knock is our sign. Jasper has always said we can never be too prepared to meet our enemies."

"In that, he was not wrong," Gavin acknowledged. "I am so damned relieved you are safe, Caro."

"I feel the same." She rose on her toes, pressing a kiss to

his lips that was slow and tentative at first, but then deepened.

Their tongues tangled. Desire sparked to a steady fire. Somehow, the rawness of the day, the danger and the relief and the love, all blended together. They became frantic. Caro clutched him to her as if she feared he would disappear should she hold him any less tightly. He held her snugly close.

They kissed until his lips ached. And still they kissed some more.

Another rap sounded at the closed door.

"No more of that until you are married, Winter," Sutton called.

Well, bloody hell.

"When can I marry you?" he whispered to Caro.

"Not soon enough," she told him, and then she pulled his head back to hers for another kiss.

Sutton knocked again, but they both ignored the sound.

EPILOGUE

Three months.
That was how long it had taken for Gavin's life to forever change.

In that time, he'd almost met his end. He'd been saved by a guardian angel who'd stolen his heart along the way. He'd lost his memory, then regained it. He'd lost sight of what was truly important, and then he'd caught it before she had slipped through his fingers. He'd married Caro Sutton.

And now, today, he had opened Winter's Boxing Academy.

He returned to the modest home he and Caro were keeping not far from some of his brothers' Mayfair townhomes to find Caro awaiting him at the door. It would take some time to get accustomed to this new life he was living, a far cry from his early days in the rookeries. But there was one aspect which required no time at all, one aspect which was natural and instinctive, fitting and so very right.

Caro.

She was still the most beautiful woman he had ever seen, and he drank in the sight of her—auburn curls framing her lovely face, an ivory gown that showed her bosom and lush curves to perfection, and a smile on her lips. But that did not mean he expected her to greet him at the door when he returned from working at the academy each day.

He drew her in his arms and stole a swift kiss, all he would allow himself for the moment. "What have you done with the household, Mrs. Winter?"

He could not lie.

He loved that she was his wife, that she wore his name, that she was *his*.

Hell, he just loved *her*.

Desperately. More with each day, in fact.

"I have given them the evening to do as they wish," she told him, her smile turning secretive. "I was hoping we might celebrate the opening of your boxing academy alone together."

He was not accustomed to having a housekeeper, a footman, a cook, and a maid. He suspected in time he would ease into the novelty. But Caro, in typical Caro fashion, knew what he needed before he did.

She helped him with his coat, hat, and gloves, the moment wonderfully intimate. He pulled her back into his arms and stole a kiss, groaning when her tongue teased his. *Damn it*, he could not make love to his wife in the entrance hall.

Could he?

The instant cockstand in his trousers told him he could.

But the gentleman in him said he ought not, even if the servants had been dismissed for the evening.

He broke the kiss, staring down at her upturned face, falling into her hazel eyes. "How was your day, my love? Have you settled your work room to your satisfaction?"

They had converted the library to become her new space. The shelf-lined walls were filled with books of her choosing, and there were plenty of tables, good natural light, and places to store her herbs and other healing materials.

"I have." She smiled. "Will you come and see?"

He kissed the tip of her nose. "Of course."

Taking his hand in hers, she led him down the hall to her work room. She had certainly put her mark upon the chamber. It was neat, tidy, and it smelled of lavender just as she did. On one of her work tables, she had pots lined up, some filled with unguents she had perfected.

"What do you think?" she asked as he made his way about.

"I think it is perfect," he said, taking her in his arms again.

The subtle swell of her belly, small but growing subtly larger with their child each day, brushed against him, reminding him of how very blessed he was. He was going to be a father, and he could not be happier.

"How was your first day at the boxing academy, my love?" She caressed his jaw, down his throat, finding the knot in his cravat and plucking at it.

"It was excellent." His cravat was undone by his wife's wicked fingers, and she was undoing the three buttons at the neck of his shirt so she could torment him by caressing the slice of his chest she had exposed. He swallowed. "Teeming with lords ready to learn from the old champion."

He had not fought another match. Recognizing he would likely never regain the full strength of his wounded arm, and in the wake of the disaster with Jones, Gavin had retired from the sport. But using his fame to attract young aristocrats desperate to practice the art of boxing had proven a boon. He had no doubt his academy would thrive, and he could not be more pleased with all the future held.

"You are happy with the academy, my love?" Her touch slid beneath his shirt, over his collarbone. "You do not wish to return to prizefighting?"

Her hand settled over his madly beating heart.

"I am happier than I could have imagined," he reassured her. "I do not want to fight any longer. All I want is to earn my keep and love my wife."

"I am glad. I want you to be happy, Gav." She pressed her mouth to his.

"I would be happier if I were making love to you," he murmured against her lips.

"No dinner?" she asked, breathless.

"Dinner can wait."

* * *

CARO TOOK her time admiring her husband as she helped him to shed his clothes. She kissed the inking he had added to his biceps. A lone C to represent her name and her place in his heart. His body was as beautiful as his heart, his chest strong and broad, covered with a light dusting of dark hair, his abdomen taut and sinewy. She kissed her way to the puckered scar of his wound, thankful for the pink, healing flesh, grateful anew that she had found him that day, and that he had lived.

They had been through so much together. But she would gladly weather all those storms again, just to have this man at her side.

"You undo me, butterfly," he said in a low voice laden with desire.

A welcoming warmth unfurled within her, settling between her thighs. "Good."

She kissed down his chest, helped him from his trousers and smalls. His cock jutted forward, long and thick and ruddy. Ready for her. She grasped him, stroking the silken length until he groaned.

"Why are you still wearing your gown, love?"

She would shed it soon enough, but first, she had another activity in mind. Caro sank to her knees before him.

"Caro," he growled.

"Hush, husband. Let me love you."

She glanced up at him from beneath lowered lashes. Holding his verdant gaze, she brought the tip of his shaft to her lips. A pearl of his mettle leaked from the slit, and she swirled her tongue over him. He was salty and musky and delicious. She sucked his cockhead, and he grew stiffer between her lips. His fingers caught her hair, holding her chignon.

"Mmm," she murmured, taking him deeper into her mouth.

His hips moved, sending him to the back of her throat. She sucked, swirled her tongue, worked him in and out of her mouth, the slide of his thickness making her desperately wet and aching. She lost herself in Gavin, inhaling the wonderful, masculine scent of him, holding his hip as she took more of his cock. But just as she brought him to the edge, he withdrew, gently pulling her to her feet.

"Off with the gown," he said thickly.

Together, they shed her gown and undergarments until she was as naked as he. Gavin sucked her greedy nipples, his fingers delving into her folds to tease her already swollen nub. She whimpered and jerked into that knowing hand, clutching at his shoulders to keep from turning into a limp puddle of lust at his feet.

He fluttered his tongue over her nipple, chuckling against her breast. "So slick and ready for me." His finger traveled down her seam, pressing against her entrance with a light, teasing touch. "You want me inside you, don't you, wife?"

"Oh yes." He gently tugged on the peak of her other breast with his teeth, sending a white-hot burst of passion soaring through her.

He slid inside her, sweetly tormenting them both. "First, I need to return the favor, love."

With that pronouncement, Gavin was on his knees. His hands were on her hips, guiding her backward until her bottom connected with the bed, and she sat perched on the edge as he caressed her inner thighs, spreading her wide. With a velvety sound of approval, he lowered his head and licked along her seam, all the way to her pulsing bud. His tongue worked over her in whisper-light licks that made her wild and desperate.

She thrust herself into his face, shamelessly seeking more. How beautiful it was, this man she loved on his knees before her, bringing her pleasure, devouring her as if she were the most decadent sweet. When he slid a long finger inside her and sucked on her pearl, she lost all control, bliss crashing over her with a potency that had her crying out. He continued licking and teasing her, drawing out her spend until she was shuddering with the power of her release.

He rose to his considerable height, then guided her to the center of the bed, his cock rigid and ready. She held her arms out to him, and he tenderly guided himself over her, taking care to balance himself on his good arm to keep his weight from her.

But she loved the feeling of him on her, warm and strong and vital. She urged him nearer, wrapping her legs around his waist as she welcomed him into her body. He slid inside with ease, filling her, stretching her. Glorious sensation exploded. Love, desire, happiness.

So much love.

They moved together, finding the rhythm that had them soaring. Their mouths met in a furiously passionate kiss as their bodies joined, and she felt in that moment they were truly one, in mind, body, spirit, heart.

She reached her pinnacle suddenly, moaning as another

crescendo of passion overwhelmed her. Gavin's thrusts quickened, and then he stiffened against her, throwing back his head and crying out as he spent. The warm rush of his seed sent a flurry of new tremors through her, drawing out the moment, the connection.

He withdrew and rolled to his side, gathering her against him and holding her there. Their hearts beat fast together, their bodies slick with perspiration. Love swelled within her, overflowing.

"I love you," he said, gently caressing her belly. "I love our little Winter, too."

She threaded her fingers through his hair, smiling. "I love you both so very much."

"Thank you." He kissed her slowly, lingeringly.

"For what?" she asked, breathless, when their mouths parted.

"For finding my sorry arse in the alley and saving me."

"Oh, Gav." She smiled, her love for him stronger than ever. "You saved me, too."

AUTHOR'S NOTE

Thank you so very much for reading *Winter's Warrior*, and thank you for loving my Winter family as much as I do. I hope Gavin and Caro's happily ever after moved you. This is goodbye *for now* to the Winter clan, but if you've enjoyed this series, then I have a feeling you're going to fall in love with the spinoff series, The Sinful Suttons. Much change is in store for the Sutton clan. For a sneak peek at Jasper Sutton and Lady Octavia's story, *Sutton's Spinster*, do read on!

Some notes on history before you turn the page…

Caro's knowledge of healing and herbs is owed to *Culpeper's English Physician and Complete Herbal*, which was first published in the seventeenth century and subsequently modified and published in various forms. I've again borrowed the cant used by the Winters and Suttons from *The Memoirs of James Hardy Vaux* (1819) and Grose's *Dictionary of the Vulgar Tongue* (1811). Bare-knuckle prizefighting was a dangerous and popular sport in the Regency era, drawing large crowds. Some fights did indeed lead to the deaths of the boxers involved. I drew inspiration from real-life prizefighters such as "Gentleman" John Jackson, who owned a boxing salon, and others such as John Gully, Tom Molyneaux, and Tom Cribb.

Now, what are you waiting for? Keep reading on for more Regency scoundrels and rogues and the daring ladies who love them…

>Until next time,
>Scarlett

PREVIEW OF SUTTON'S SPINSTER

*J*asper Sutton, London's most dedicated scoundrel, needs a wife. He needs one quickly. He needs one yesterday, in fact. His requirements are precise. She has to be capable of mothering the wild twin daughters who have unexpectedly appeared in his life. She must also possess the patience of a saint and the understanding of an angel. Better still if she is plain and has no expectation of a true marriage. He is not about to reform his ways. But how is he to find such a paragon of womanly virtue when a troublesome, maddening baggage keeps haunting his gaming hell and getting herself into scrapes?

Lady Octavia Alexander, the ton's most dedicated spinster, has no need of a husband. She is quite firmly and happily on the shelf, a devoted aunt to her beloved nieces and nephews. But she does harbor one illicit dream: she wants to start her own newspaper devoted solely to scandal and gossip. What better way to do so than to immerse herself in the sordid underworld of the East End? There is just one problem standing in the way of her plans, and his name is Jasper Sutton. But Octavia won't abandon her independence and her future for an unscrupulous rogue. No matter how handsome he is, and regardless of how irresistible his kisses.

Between running his family's gaming hell, chasing after his wayward daughters, and keeping Lady Octavia from being robbed, spirited away by some enterprising criminal, or worse, Jasper is losing his patience. Even more concerning? He's beginning to fear the only woman he truly *wants* to marry is the vexing lady who has sworn she will never wed. All he has to do is change her mind and win her heart.

* * *

Chapter One

Not bloody *again*.

Jasper Sutton's booted foot had connected with something soft as he seated himself at the desk in his office at The Sinner's Palace. The gaming hell he and his siblings owned together was teeming with drunken lords. The hour was despicably late by anyone's standards, even for a voluptuary such as himself. He wanted gin and he wanted quim, and not necessarily in that order.

What he did *not* want was one of his twin daughters hiding beneath his desk when she was supposed to be abed.

"Elizabeth," he guessed, for she was undeniably the naughtiest of the two children who had been unexpectedly delivered to his hell a fortnight ago.

Abandoned was a better fucking word for what their mother—whomever she was—had done. That was the trouble with possessing an insatiable appetite for rutting. Sooner or later, the rutting produced brats.

And sometimes, the mothers of the brats decided they did

not want the burden of extra mouths to feed. And also sometimes, the mothers abandoned their daughters on the steps of a gaming hell at dawn and left them there for any despicable bastard to abuse, without a thought or a care. Until, *thank the Lord*, his men had arrived and taken the girls within before something had befallen them.

Jasper had always tried to take care to avoid siring a bastard. But he could admit the resemblance the children bore to him was apparent. Black hair, hazel Sutton eyes, the dent in his chin. There had been nights when he had been too deep in his cups to know where he'd spent his seed.

And now, he had daughters to look after. Twin devilish imps who were six years old and filled with mischief.

Still, no child emerged or responded. He tapped the girlish lump beneath his desk with the tip of his boot. "Anne?"

The rustle of fabric met his ears, followed by two sets of giggles.

Christ. The both of them were at it tonight. Sinner that he was, he sent a silent prayer for patience heavenward. And then with a scowl, he rose from his chair and hunkered down to peer beneath the massive piece of furniture which had only recently been repaired after a pistol had blown a portion of it apart. Two sets of grins and hazel eyes greeted him.

"Girls," he chastised sternly, "you are meant to be sleeping. What the devil are you doing hiding beneath my desk at this time of the evening?"

"We miss playing 'idey," Elizabeth announced, unrepentant.

Hidey, as he had come to learn, was a game his daughters had established to enliven their evenings when one of their mother's gentlemen callers paid a visit.

"Ma always told us it were fun to 'ide when the gentlemen arrived," Anne added brightly.

It was clear their mother had been a Covent Garden nun. Could have been one of the doxies employed by The Sinner's Palace for the entertainments of his patrons. Could have been someone else. The girls said her name was Ma Bellington.

Bellington was a right fancy name for an East End whore. He suspected the woman had never told their daughters her true name, as Bellington did not mean a thing to him. Not that he expected it to. There had been occasions when he had not bothered to exchange names with his bedmates, it was true.

He wasn't proud of his past now that he was older and wiser. But he'd been a reckless, wild rakehell in his youth. No denying it. Just as there was no denying these hellions were his.

"Out from under the desk," he ordered the twins sternly. "We've talked about this before, no?"

"We wasn't tired," Elizabeth announced, crawling from beneath the desk in her nightdress and standing to eye him balefully. "It's right dull 'ere, it is."

Anne emerged from beneath the desk as well, frowning. "I told Lizbeth I didn't want to do it, but she made me."

He sighed. It had only taken him hours to discover that Elizabeth was the twin who delighted in galloping all over the hell, leaving mischief in her wake, and asking him so many questions he feared his head might explode like a melon tossed from a roof. Anne had a saucy disposition, was quick to turn into a watering pot, and liked to blame everything on her sister.

"What did I tell you yesterday when I caught you hiding beneath the hazard table?" he asked with as much calm as he could muster.

He'd been furious at the sight of his children wandering about the gaming hell, disrupting confused patrons. The discovery had made his need of a wife—someone to tame and look after his wayward offspring—all the more apparent.

"You said we couldn't go where the fancy coves be," Elizabeth said.

"You didn't say nothing about your desk," Anne added mulishly.

Before he could address either of them, a knock sounded on the door. Three raps in quick succession, which signified *more* trouble.

"Christ," he muttered.

"That's the Lord," Anne told him.

"I am aware," he said, silently praying for strength. And patience. And strength.

"You owe 'im an apology," Elizabeth announced with a superior air.

Sodding hell. "*Apology*, Elizabeth," he corrected.

"What's sodding mean?" Anne asked.

Damnation. Had he said that bit aloud? To his utter shame, he discovered that he—Jasper Sutton, scourge of the East End—was bloody *flushing*.

He coughed to cover his embarrassment and called out to Hugh, who was on door duty this evening. "What is it now?"

"*She's* returned," Hugh called, his tone grim.

Jasper did not need to ask who his man was speaking of. Over the last few months, one woman had continually appeared, ignoring his warnings, his threats—hell, even his kisses.

Lady Octavia Alexander.

And damn him if the mere name of the dark-haired beauty did not make his cock twitch to life. Until he recalled his children were still standing before him.

Children.

His.

He was yet growing accustomed to this abrupt change of circumstances.

"Tell her to go back to Mayfair where she damned well belongs," he ordered Hugh, for he had far more important matters awaiting him this evening.

Namely, the twins who had once more escaped from their shared room to wander about unattended.

The door burst open, and Lady Octavia crossed the threshold, elegant, beautiful, and maddening as hell. Her vividly blue eyes settled upon him first, and how he despised the bolt of lust that hit him. So, too, the memories of the frantic kisses they had shared, her tongue in his mouth.

The minx.

Christ, she was delicious.

And infuriating.

And delicious.

Damnation.

"You are not welcome here, Lady Octavia," he told her, just as he had on numerous occasions in the past. "I will have one of my men escort you back to the safety of your sister's home."

"Children, Sutton?" she asked, her gaze flitting from his daughters, to him, then back again.

"Aye," he ground out. "Children. *Mine.*"

She had not trespassed at The Sinner's Palace in three weeks. Not that he had been counting. And not that he had missed her irritating intrusions. Because he most certainly had not.

Her mouth dropped open. Pretty, pink, lush mouth. Not a spinster's mouth at all, and that bothered him for reasons he didn't care to examine. Lady Octavia Alexander had no desire to marry. All she wanted was to be at the helm of a gossip journal. Hers, of course. When she had initially approached him with the idea, he had laughed. And then he had kissed her senseless. And then *she* had been the one laughing.

The bloody nuisance.

"*Your* children," she repeated at last.

"Mine," he said again, willing her to go away.

To go far, far away.

To the continent, in fact.

Or mayhap the Americas.

Out of his reach, wherever that took her.

Was the moon a possibility?

"You are a father."

"Aye," he gritted, frowning at her. "Are you daft, woman? I've just said so."

He was being rude, and he knew it. Also, he did not care.

"Don't say *daft*," he added as an afterthought, addressing his wide-eyed daughters.

"I would never," Anne breathed. "It would be unkind, Papa."

Papa. His cold, dead heart never failed to warm at the title, and curse him if he knew why. He'd certainly not wanted spawn. Still didn't want them. Not particularly. They were trouble, these two.

Hence his need for a wife.

Yesterday.

A plain, appreciative woman without expectations who was willing to guide his children and turn a blind eye to whatever the hell he wished to do that did not involve her.

Lady Octavia was grinning at him like the cat who'd got into the cream. "Yes, Papa. It is most *unkind* to call a lady who has only ever been polite to you *daft*."

"Do not call me Papa," he growled at her, stalking forward.

Toward her.

Pulled.

Always, always pulled. This woman was vexing and she was intoxicating, and he wanted more of her, and he wanted her to go away and never to return.

But mostly, he wanted more of her.

"Papa?" asked one of his daughters, and he was ashamed to admit that with them at his back, he could not distinguish one voice from the next.

He paused, stopping just short of Lady Octavia. "What is it now, daughter?" he asked, casting a glance over his shoulder.

"I want a cat," Anne said.

"I want a dog," Elizabeth announced.

"Then you shall have both," Lady Octavia proclaimed, her voice cheerful, benevolent.

Annoying.

He turned back to her, pinning her with a glare. "Hold your tongue, Lady Octavia."

She winked, the outrageous baggage. "Force me to if you dare."

Challenge accepted, milady.

He would have great fun with her tongue. Later. Not with his children as an audience. Kisses could wait. Anne and Elizabeth needed to get to bed…

Want more? Get *Sutton's Spinster*!

DON'T MISS SCARLETT'S OTHER
ROMANCES!

Complete Book List
HISTORICAL ROMANCE

Heart's Temptation
A Mad Passion (Book One)
Rebel Love (Book Two)
Reckless Need (Book Three)
Sweet Scandal (Book Four)
Restless Rake (Book Five)
Darling Duke (Book Six)
The Night Before Scandal (Book Seven)

Wicked Husbands
Her Errant Earl (Book One)
Her Lovestruck Lord (Book Two)
Her Reformed Rake (Book Three)
Her Deceptive Duke (Book Four)
Her Missing Marquess (Book Five)
Her Virtuous Viscount (Book Six)

DON'T MISS SCARLETT'S OTHER ROMANCES!

League of Dukes
Nobody's Duke (Book One)
Heartless Duke (Book Two)
Dangerous Duke (Book Three)
Shameless Duke (Book Four)
Scandalous Duke (Book Five)
Fearless Duke (Book Six)

Notorious Ladies of London
Lady Ruthless (Book One)
Lady Wallflower (Book Two)
Lady Reckless (Book Three)
Lady Wicked (Book Four)
Lady Lawless (Book Five)

The Wicked Winters
Wicked in Winter (Book One)
Wedded in Winter (Book Two)
Wanton in Winter (Book Three)
Wishes in Winter (Book 3.5)
Willful in Winter (Book Four)
Wagered in Winter (Book Five)
Wild in Winter (Book Six)
Wooed in Winter (Book Seven)
Winter's Wallflower (Book Eight)
Winter's Woman (Book Nine)
Winter's Whispers (Book Ten)
Winter's Waltz (Book Eleven)
Winter's Widow (Book Twelve)
Winter's Warrior (Book Thirteen)

The Sinful Suttons
Sutton's Spinster (Book One)

DON'T MISS SCARLETT'S OTHER ROMANCES!

Stand-alone Novella
Lord of Pirates

CONTEMPORARY ROMANCE
Love's Second Chance
Reprieve (Book One)
Perfect Persuasion (Book Two)
Win My Love (Book Three)

Coastal Heat
Loved Up (Book One)

ABOUT THE AUTHOR

USA Today and Amazon bestselling author Scarlett Scott writes steamy Victorian and Regency romance with strong, intelligent heroines and sexy alpha heroes. She lives in Pennsylvania and Maryland with her Canadian husband, adorable identical twins, and one TV-loving dog.

A self-professed literary junkie and nerd, she loves reading anything, but especially romance novels, poetry, and Middle English verse. Catch up with her on her website http://www.scarlettscottauthor.com/. Hearing from readers never fails to make her day.

Scarlett's complete book list and information about upcoming releases can be found at http://www.scarlettscottauthor.com/.

Connect with Scarlett! You can find her here:
 Join Scarlett Scott's reader's group on Facebook for early excerpts, giveaways, and a whole lot of fun!
 Sign up for her newsletter here.
 Follow Scarlett on Amazon
 Follow Scarlett on BookBub
 www.instagram.com/scarlettscottauthor/
 www.twitter.com/scarscoromance
 www.pinterest.com/scarlettscott
 www.facebook.com/AuthorScarlettScott

Printed in Dunstable, United Kingdom